Telegrams
and
Teacakes

ALSO BY AMY MILLER

Heartaches and Christmas Cakes
Wartime Brides and Wedding Cakes

Amy Miller

Telegrams
and
Teacakes

Bookouture

Published by Bookouture in 2018

An imprint of StoryFire Ltd.

Carmelite House
50 Victoria Embankment
London EC4Y 0DZ

www.bookouture.com

ISBN: 978-1-78681-539-2
eBook ISBN: 978-1-78681-538-5

'No one is useless in this world who lightens the burdens of another.'
- Charles Dickens

Spring 1942

Chapter One

Though the small terraced house in Queen Street was half-collapsed, with bricks and broken furniture spewing onto the pavement, it was impossibly hard for Betty Mitchell to say farewell. Her hopes and dreams, she thought, as she gaped at her bombed-out home one last time, had literally been reduced to rubble. The house that she'd once loved now resembled a doll's house that had been ripped in half and stamped on. The upstairs bedroom was half-intact, the marital bed upended at a hair-raising angle against a backdrop of floral wallpaper. Broken fragments of her wedding gift teapot and crockery lay in the dust. The smell of burning lingered, and if she closed her eyes for a second, the backs of her eyelids filled with flames. After months of standing like this, abandoned and precarious, the house would soon be demolished. All traces of her life would be eradicated, which was – Betty had bravely convinced herself – for the best.

'This is all your fault, Robert Mitchell,' she muttered to nobody, lifting her moist eyes to the sky, which bulged with rainclouds. Thinking about what she'd secretly discovered about her husband, Robert, after their house had been bombed by the Luftwaffe months earlier, she was resigned to the fact that she had no choice but to disappear. Gulping back tears at the memory of the sight, which had felt like a knife through the heart, she swallowed hard and wrapped her arms round her narrow waist. Despite being tiny, at just under five feet tall and as thin as a reed, she was going to have to be stronger than she had ever been. Her life in Bristol was over. She was going to wipe the slate clean and start again, in a new town where nobody knew her name. In the chaos of wartime, with swathes of the population evacuated out of cities to safer areas in the countryside or on the coast, she would have to erase all memory of her former life as if it was a spelling mistake in a school exercise book.

She blinked away the tears in her grey eyes and tucked her long honey-blonde hair behind her ears with trembling hands, then stared in horror as a large brown rat scuttled into a mangled bread bin in the pile of bricks before her. She pushed her toe into a pile of gravel.

'More rats than people round here now,' piped up Frankie, one of her neighbours, who, in among the debris of her own house, was erecting a sign appealing for scrap metal for munitions, in aid of the Red Cross.

'Are you not working today?' she went on. 'Haven't seen that husband of yours in a while. At the docks, is he?'

Betty smiled sadly and smoothed down her blue day dress that had been patched and darned more times than she cared to admit. At breakfast that morning her pale complexion had burned scarlet when she'd told Robert and his great-uncle, with whom they were staying, that she was working a long shift at the tobacco factory and wouldn't be back until late. She'd expected Robert to look up from his porridge, slam his rough hand on the kitchen table, look into her eyes and accuse her of lying, but he simply stirred more than his fair share of sweetened condensed milk into his tea and nodded. In truth, of course, Betty hadn't gone into the factory at all, but had instead sent a scrawled handwritten note to her superior to say she was unwell with a high fever.

'I'm not due in today,' she lied to Frankie, before shrugging. 'And Robert is… well, he's an essential worker, isn't he? All the dockers are part of a scheme where they'll go wherever their labour is needed, so I don't know where he'll be from one day to the next.'

Registering the irony of her own words, Betty tried to keep the emotion from her voice, before sighing. 'Let's just say he's keeping busy,' she finished with a shrug.

'Course he is,' said Frankie. 'Everyone's busy with the business of just surviving. Every day I come back here, and more bits and bobs have been looted, and nobody's doing a thing about it! It's as if all the rules have been turned on their head since this war started, ain't it, lovey?'

Betty nodded, taking one last glance at her old house, now a flattened dream, and said goodbye before Frankie could ask any more questions.

She walked briskly towards Stapleton Road railway station with a pounding heart and one word on her lips: *Bournemouth*. She'd been there on a seaside trip once as a child, with the orphanage, and remembered how the sea had glittered like an open jewellery box and the ice cream had melted in the sun faster than she could lick. It would be as good a place as any.

She had been unable to bring luggage with her and had only a liver-paste sandwich, a pair of sharp sewing scissors, one change of clothes, her identity card, gas mask case and Robert's life savings stuffed into her small bag. There was enough money to get her a train ticket to Bournemouth and pay rent for new digs for a month or two. Course, she'd need a job, but she was a hard worker and would quickly prove herself wherever help was needed.

Approaching the impressive station building, Betty passed row upon row of houses that, like her own home, had been destroyed by heavy bombing. She stared in surprise at an old man who was boiling up soup on an open fire. *Of course*, she thought, *the gas mains have been destroyed*. He gave her a cheerful wave and she waved back.

'Luck be with you,' she whispered. The people of Bristol were undeniably ingenious and resilient but lives everywhere had been turned upside down and shaken about. It was as if they were all living inside a broken snow globe. Frankie was right: the rules *had* changed. You only had to think about the moon to realise that. Before the war Betty had adored the romance of moonlit nights in the city, but during the Blitz she had come to dread moonlight because the moon's reflection on the River Avon gave the Luftwaffe a guide to the heart of Bristol, like traitorous torchlight. Night after night she'd prayed for cloud and rain, a cloak of darkness to hide under. And of course, before the war, Betty had believed Robert was a fine, upstanding, dependable husband whose heart was as strong and capable of love as his hands were of hard physical labour. A husband she could trust with her whole self, and who cherished her as he'd so passionately proclaimed on their wedding day. How bitterly wrong she had been. Well, she thought as she arrived at the railway station platform, where girls were waving their handkerchiefs to their sweethearts through a veil of steam, now it was *her* turn to break the rules.

Chapter Two

Blinking in amazement as a small loaf flew across the bakery, skimming the noses of a queue of astonished customers, Audrey Barton didn't know whether to laugh or cry. Britain was in the midst of the third year of a seemingly never-ending war with Germany, but this morning Barton's bakery shop was a battleground. Blushing at some of the ripe language erupting from the customers' mouths as the bread landed with a thud on the black and white tiled floor, Audrey tucked her hair into her bakery cap, then rested her hand on the swell of her pregnant stomach as she eased herself out from behind the wooden shop counter.

'Ladies!' she said, stamping her wooden clog on the floor, before raising flat palms in the air. 'Please, calm yourselves.'

'You won't catch me eating that grey muck!' Flo, one of Audrey's regular customers, said, dusting off her hands, after throwing the bread. 'Why, after all the years I've been coming here, are you selling bread that tastes like sawdust? If your Charlie were here, he wouldn't allow you to use that black flour!'

Audrey sighed at the mention of her darling husband Charlie, who was away fighting overseas. She missed him dearly and painfully. Keeping the bakery going in his absence had been a challenge and wasn't getting easier, especially now she was heavily pregnant. She winced as the baby growing in her belly elbowed her in the ribs, as if to say: 'That woman needs a flea in her ear! Tell her what for!' Audrey sighed. Flo was objecting to the government's introduction of the National Loaf – a 14oz loaf of bread made with wheatmeal flour with the bran left in – which, thanks to significant British shipping losses, bakers nationwide were now obliged to bake instead of the usual selection of white loaves.

'Even the Royal Family have to eat the National Loaf,' soothed Audrey. 'And even if he was here, Charlie wouldn't be able to change the regulations. We don't have any choice. Sliced white bread is illegal now except under special licence. The local bread officers regularly inspect us to make sure we're doing what we're supposed to be doing. Would you rather see me behind bars?'

Audrey knelt to retrieve the loaf from the floor. Wasting food was now a punishable offence – just last week a Bournemouth woman had been fined £3 for wasting a whole fresh loaf – so the Barton household would have this loaf for tea, spread thinly with creamed margarine and home-made jam.

'Rate we're going, we'll be surviving on peas and porridge come winter,' Flo said. 'Mark my words.'

'There are sacrifices one has to make in wartime, Flo, and this is one of them,' said Elizabeth, another bakery customer. 'If you're that desperate, why don't you sieve the wheatmeal flour through your nylon stockings and bake your own white bread?'

Several women in the queue laughed, while Flo remained indignant.

'Mind you, who's got nylon stockings to spare these days?' continued Elizabeth. 'I've been making do with gravy browning on my legs in place of nylons for months. I'm beginning to feel more like a brisket of beef than a woman!'

The women in the queue cracked up laughing again, but Elizabeth held her finger to her lips, lowered her voice and pointed outside to where a group of smart and dashing American soldiers, newly billeted in the town, stood in the sunshine in Fisherman's Road, smoking Camel cigarettes. Two of them held either end of a long rope stretched across the width of the road. With smiles on their faces they swung the rope round and round, so that no fewer than eight of the local children could skip, all the while chanting: 'Got any gum, chum?' before exploding into giggles.

'You know where you could get some new nylons from though, don't you, Flo?' Elizabeth whispered, her eyes on a gaggle of young women in the street who stood close to the American GIs, trying to attract their attention. Audrey sighed again. Though the American soldiers were already a popular addition to the town, for being fun, rich and for handing out chewing gum, candy, Coca-Cola and nylons to girls, some young women were dropping at their feet to such an extent they were already getting a name for themselves as 'Yankee bags'. Audrey didn't blame those young women for wanting to attend their parties and have some fun during the bleak wartime evenings, but she suspected some would throw caution to the wind and regret it later. War was like that – it made people live like there might not be a tomorrow. Her stepsister Lily's illegitimate child was testament to that.

'What do you reckon, Flo?' persisted Elizabeth. 'Shall I ask one of those boys for you?'

'I'm not putting up with this whiffle-whaffle a moment longer,' Flo said. 'I don't want free nylons. I want a white oven-bottom loaf, with a beautiful golden crust, that's soft and light to the touch. A loaf that smells so good and is so warm still that you can't resist pulling at it as you walk home, so it looks like a squirrel's been at it! You know what I mean, Audrey. The lovely bread you've baked for years that's so good you don't even need butter on it. I want my usual loaf and I won't leave until I get one!'

With that Flo sat down heavily on the wooden chair Audrey kept in the shop for the older ladies to rest their legs, folding her arms across her chest. Audrey rested her hand on Flo's shoulder.

'What's really the matter?' said Audrey. 'I know this can't be about the bread. We'll have white again one day. Is it your sons? Have you heard from them?'

Flo shook her bowed head and fat tears dripped down her cheeks. Her twin boys were in the Royal Navy and last time Audrey had asked, she hadn't heard from them in months. Just like all the women in the queue whose lives were touched in some way by the war, it was sometimes too difficult to 'keep calm and carry on' as the Prime Minister Winston Churchill repeatedly ordered on the wireless.

'Not a word,' said Flo quietly. 'Every time I see the messenger boy delivering telegrams round our way I'm convinced it'll be me next. I'm beginning to fear that they're in one of those filthy prisoner-of-war camps, or that they're badly injured in a field hospital or that nobody has noticed that they're…'

Audrey's stomach turned over as Flo swallowed and left her unfinished sentence hanging in the air. Though some women heard from their menfolk every week, others rarely got word and Audrey herself hadn't heard from Charlie, who was somewhere in the Mediterranean, for weeks. He wasn't the type of man to write often, but she wished he'd send word. Despite convincing herself on a daily basis that 'no news is good news', fear followed her around like a shadow. Some days she couldn't even look at their wedding photograph because it upset her too much.

'You would have got word if they'd been captured or were injured,' said Audrey. 'I should imagine it's just difficult for them to write. Someone was telling me it can take more than a month for mail to get out. Who knows what they are up against on a daily basis? If my William's injuries are anything to go by, writing a letter home isn't going to be a priority.'

Audrey was referring to her brother William's war wounds after his truck was hit by an incendiary bomb while fighting in France: horrific burn scars across one side of his face and a foot so badly injured it had been amputated. Not to mention the mental scars, invisible to the eye but ever present. She and Flo exchanged concerned glances and the other customers in the queue murmured and nodded their heads, thinking about their own loved ones who they were praying were safe.

Everyone was absolutely sick to death of the war and the worst thing was the not knowing. Every time you opened the newspaper or listened to the wireless, there was news of another part of the world ripped to shreds by the war. British troops were in Japan, there was a campaign in Libya and a battle in Russia – it was hard to keep up.

'Perhaps you're right,' said Flo. 'I just keep hoping for some good news.'

Audrey nodded. Though for Bournemouth, after the horrific months of the Blitz the previous year, the dreaded air raids had eased off slightly, people were still having to dig deeper than ever to stay cheerful. Rations made life hard, no petrol was permitted unless for emergency, firesides had to be shared with neighbours to save on fuel, bathing was restricted to no more than five inches of hot water per bath and clothing coupons were down. It was tough to be optimistic, even for Audrey, whose reason for living was to keep her customers and her family happy. But with no word from Charlie since she'd written to tell him about her pregnancy, and with her favourite shop girl Maggie gone to London to be near her new husband George's family, she was missing the pre-war days. She wished she had paid more attention to the simple happiness of peacetime. Peace itself was a reason to celebrate and she'd taken it for granted. Now, it seemed that every day turned up a new set of problems. She needed a new shop girl to replace Maggie, the customers didn't much like the new National Loaf and she couldn't even create the celebration cakes she so loved to bake because the Food Minister, Lord Woolton, had banned the sale of iced cakes. There was no denying it – being cheery was a challenge. You just had to be grateful for small mercies: a sunny day, a night without an air raid, an extra rasher of bacon from the butcher.

'We could *all* do with some good news,' said Audrey wistfully, patting Flo's shoulder before returning to her post behind the counter. 'That's for sure.'

Audrey's attention was caught by her stepsister Lily, who had lived at the bakery since she'd arrived on the doorstep pregnant out of wedlock over a year ago, loudly clearing her throat. Standing in front of the floral curtain that led through to the bakehouse out back, her face was lit with the brightest smile, showing off the signature 'lucky' gap between her front teeth, her copper hair glowing in a halo around her head. Audrey was continually taken aback by Lily's natural beauty.

'*I've* got some good news,' said Lily, clutching a telegram in her hand, her cheeks flushed bright pink and her blue eyes glassy with tears. She put her other hand to her throat and fiddled with the locket on a chain she wore. 'You won't believe what I've just heard, Audrey,' she said. 'I can hardly believe it myself. I feel quite peculiar.'

Chapter Three

In the waiting room at the railway station, where the wall clock ticked loudly, Betty had locked herself into the ladies' room and pulled the sewing scissors from her bag. Sitting perched on the closed toilet seat, she balanced her compact mirror on the mottled brown Bakelite door handle and got to work, chopping eight inches from her long honey-blonde hair, until she had a short jaw-length bob. Twisting her head this way and that, she realised it was a little uneven and longer on one side, but with a headscarf, it would do. She'd never been one for make-up but had the remains of an old Pillarbox Red lipstick in her bag, so she applied the colour to her lips, pinched her cheeks and stared at her new self. At twenty-four years old she was relatively young, but after six years of marriage to Robert she felt twice her age. Thinking of Robert, she straightened her fingers and glanced down at her wedding band. When he first proposed, a month after they started courting, they'd stood at the glistening window of Simpson's Jewellers and he'd promised to buy her a pink cluster ring, soon as he'd saved enough wages. She had believed everything he said. Of course, the fancy ring never materialised. Not that she cared about jewels. It was a family she'd wanted, babies and children to fill their hearts and marital home with love and laughter, but Robert always had a reason for why they should wait. Before the war it was because his wages weren't good enough. Since the war had started, it was the uncertainty he blamed. He would listen to the wireless and shake his head, before telling her, 'This is no world for kiddies to come into.' Now she knew why. Loosening the ring from her finger, she stood up and lifted the toilet lid, holding the ring above the pan.

Shall I?, she mused, imagining the ring sinking into the sewers and catching on a rat's tail, before thinking better of it.

I'll sell it, she thought, stuffing it into her purse along with the lengths of hair she'd cut from her head. Making her way out of the ladies', half-expecting people to point and laugh at her new look, she walked quickly to the platform to await the train. It was buzzing with military personnel and sweethearts saying goodbye to one another after short bursts of precious leave. It was hard not to stare.

As she boarded the train, Betty tried to distract herself by reading a copy of the *Bournemouth Echo* that had been left in the luggage rack. Scanning the Situations Vacant page, her eyes rested on a position for a shop girl in a bakery. She carefully tore out the advertisement, folded it up and put it in her purse. As soon as she arrived in Bournemouth, she would go to the bakery and put herself forward for the job and if that didn't work, she'd get a job as a domestic help. Anything would do.

Gazing out of the window at the blurred scenery, she tried to control her rising panic as her thoughts turned to Robert and how he would react when she didn't return home tonight. While his uncle sat reading the paper, or polishing his collection of horse brasses, would Robert peer out of the window criss-crossed with Splinternet tape, scanning the street with concern for her safety? Or would he slip out of the back door, as he so often did, and disappear into the night like a furtive fox?

Doris is welcome to him, she told herself, digging her nails into her palms.

Betty remembered the painful evening when she'd followed him, wondering where it was that he went every other evening. She had suspected that he was going to the King's Head pub and was horrified when he went instead to an address in Hamlyn Street and was lovingly greeted by Doris, a girl she'd been at school with.

Wearing a mop hat and apron, Doris clutched a baby in her arms while a toddler and an older boy twisted around her ankles.

Betty had almost collapsed on the pavement when the toddler had held up his arms to Robert and called him 'Dadda'. It had taken only a simple enquiry, door-knocking Doris's elderly neighbour and pretending to be lost, to discover that Robert had another family. Another wife! Doris and Robert were husband and wife. They had children together. His life with Betty was a lie. Her marriage was a sham.

What a silly girl I've been, she thought as the train slowed down as it drew closer to Bournemouth Central station. Suddenly furious, she pushed down the train window, reached into her purse and hurled the gold ring out onto the tracks. As soon as the shiny band landed on the stony ground, a magpie deftly swooped down from a tree and pinched it for its nest.

'More fool you,' Betty said, slamming the window shut and gathering her few things, ready to disembark – but not before the old ominous rhyme passed through her head. *One for sorrow, two for joy…* With trembling legs and a pounding heart, she stepped onto the station platform, quickly scanning the horizon for another magpie. But there was only one visible in the cloudless sky. A shiver ran up her spine: *one for sorrow.*

*

Lily read the telegram several times over in her head before clearing her throat and looking up at Audrey's face, which, since she had fallen pregnant, glowed a shade of fireside pink whether it was hot or cold.

'What is it?' asked Audrey, her hands on her hips and her blue eyes widening. 'Don't keep me waiting! Who's the telegram from?'

Lily swallowed. She looked around the bakery shop that had become her home since she turned up on the doorstep, secretly pregnant by her cheating boss and with nowhere to go. On the first day she'd arrived, Audrey had taken her to help at the Bournemouth School for Boys, where French soldiers who had been rescued from the beaches at Dunkirk were being cared for, and she had met Jacques – a young French soldier. The two of them had instantly liked each other and when Jacques returned to active service, he'd written Lily a beautiful letter declaring his love for her. But, before she had been able to reply and confess to him that she was in fact pregnant by another man, Jacques' mother had written to inform her and Audrey that Jacques was missing at sea and presumed killed. Now though, more than a year later, Jacques himself had written to Lily to tell her that he had in fact been in a prisoner-of-war camp, but he had escaped.

'It's Jacques,' she said, her voice almost a whisper as the enormity of the news sank into her brain. Audrey gasped, her hand flying to cover her mouth. Though the bakery family had only known Jacques for a few days, their lives had been touched by his courage and integrity. They had all been devastated to hear that he was presumed dead.

'Jacques?' said Audrey, lifting her hands to her cheeks in shock. 'Alive?'

'Yes, he's alive,' said Lily, blinking in disbelief. 'He says—'

The words stuck in her throat and she stopped talking. Audrey grabbed Lily's hand and squeezed it. Lily's eyes lowered to the telegram, the few words blurring in front of her eyes as she took a deep breath and began to read, her voice trembling with excitement and shock.

I am alive. I escaped a camp. You have been my reason to survive. Please write. Jacques.

Lily raised her head to meet Audrey's gaze.

'I need to sit down,' said Audrey. 'Goodness me, Lily. Isn't that wonderful news? What a thing!'

Lily nodded, genuinely utterly delighted; but already, in a distant part of her mind, fear was gathering like rainclouds. Jacques had said that she was his reason for surviving, but he didn't know that she had a child. He had never known that when they had met, she was actually pregnant out of wedlock – a fact that had brought great shame to her family. Would he still like her when he learned that she was bringing up Joy on her own? It was extremely unlikely, wasn't it? For a moment she stayed quiet, but Audrey immediately seemed to read her mind and pulled her in for a tight hug.

'In wartime life gets complicated,' she said quietly, and gently released her stepsister from her arms. 'He knows that, probably better than anyone.'

'But how can I tell him?' Lily replied. 'He has a picture of me in his head that isn't true. How can I reply to this?'

Lily's initial happiness at receiving the telegram was still burning in her belly, but the thought of shattering Jacques' dream was unbearable. If the idea of Lily had helped him survive the grimmest experience of his life, what would happen when he discovered that idea was all wrong – that she wasn't the innocent girl he imagined her to be?

'Any man worth his salt will understand that you made a brave decision,' Audrey said. 'At the very least, you must give him the opportunity to understand. You clearly mean so much to him, so you must tell him the truth. In my experience truth will out. It always does. Better slip with foot than tongue. Try not to worry, Lily. This telegram is a reason to celebrate.'

'Yes, you're right,' replied Lily with a smile, but their conversation was interrupted by the gentle jingle of the shop bell as a young woman walked in from the street. Blinking, Lily wiped the tears of joy from her eyes, folded up the letter, stuffed it into her pocket and smiled at the woman. She was very petite and pretty, but dressed in a blue day dress that had seen better days, its fabric so thin it was almost translucent. Her hair was cut in the most peculiar way, with one side slightly longer than the other. She had grey bags under her grey eyes and seemed nervous, checking over her shoulder as if worried someone might be following her. With a bag on one arm and her gas mask case on the other, she held a torn piece of newspaper in her hand.

'How can I help you?' asked Audrey, resuming her place behind the counter. The girl straightened her back and lifted her chin, before clearing her throat.

'I've come about the job I saw advertised in the *Echo*,' she said, holding up the torn sheet of newspaper.

'Yes,' said Audrey. 'It's still available. I'm looking for someone to start immediately.'

'I'm hard-working and honest and I won't let you down,' the girl said. 'I've worked in a shop and a factory and I've never missed a shift. I've been volunteering for the WVS too, with collections and their canteen. I like to be busy and useful.'

Lily looked at Audrey. She came out from behind the counter and shook Betty warmly by the hand.

'What's your name, love?' Audrey said. 'Are you from around here? I don't recognise your face.'

'It's Betty,' she said, her eyes darting around the shop for a good few moments as she hesitated before she spoke again. 'I'm Betty… Smith… and I'm from… Portsmouth.'

'Okay,' said Audrey, frowning slightly and exchanging glances with Lily. 'Do you have references please, Betty?'

Panic swept over Betty's features and Audrey, who Lily knew couldn't bear to put people on the spot and watch anyone suffer, gently patted her hand. 'Never mind about those,' she said quickly. 'What good is a piece of paper anyway? I'll need to see for myself how you work and interact with the customers, maybe do some deliveries too to the folk who can't get to the shop. I'm looking for someone who will always put the customer first, even if their feet and shoulders are aching. Since my husband, the master baker, joined up and our shop girl, Maggie left, we're a small team, but we get the job done. Women have stepped up to the mark on the buses, trams, railways, on the land and in the munitions factories – and we're no exception in Barton's.'

Betty smiled.

'Folk round here rely on our bread,' explained Audrey. 'In times of rationing, it's helping to keep the wolf from the door and is a staple of people's diets, so your job here would be very important indeed. We all take pride in the bakery, so I hope you would too.'

Betty nodded enthusiastically. 'Yes, Mrs Barton,' she said. 'Of course.'

'Well, I'd be willing to give you a two-day trial, starting tomorrow,' said Audrey. 'Why don't you come back later, for dinner?'

'Oh no, I couldn't put you out,' Betty said.

'A slice of cake then?' Audrey said. 'I'm baking a honey cake for the occasion. I'm friends with the bee-keeper, you see. Come round this evening, you wouldn't be putting me out. It would be an opportunity to meet everyone you'll be working with and my mother-in-law Pat, who is heavily involved in the WVS. She'll direct you to where you're needed most.'

Audrey paused for a moment before quickly stuffing a paper bag with two scones.

'Please take these with you,' she said. 'They're nothing much, just stales.'

'They're not sta—' started Lily, but Audrey shut her down with a glare and pushed the scones into Betty's hands.

'Thank you,' Betty said in amazement. 'That's so generous. Are you sure about later? You don't even know me. I don't want to be a burden.'

'There's a place at my table for an honest hard worker,' said Audrey. 'And I can see by your hands and the soles of your shoes that you're not an idle girl. It nearly slipped my mind but we're doing some clothes-swapping and sewing this evening too. Aren't we, Lily?'

'Are we?' said Lily, frowning. 'Oh yes, we are.'

Betty's face reddened.

'Oh,' said Betty. 'But I don't have any clothes to swap. I haven't brought very much with me, I travelled light since most of my clothes were lost in air raids…'

Audrey waved her hands in the air dismissively.

'Don't let that worry you,' she said. 'We can sort that out.'

Betty gave a small, gratified smile, her eyes flickering nervously from Lily to Audrey. There was something she was hiding, that was plain to see, but Lily knew Audrey would get to the bottom of it – she had a nose for the truth. While Audrey saw Betty out of the shop, Lily's thoughts returned to the telegram from Jacques that burned a hole in her pocket. She wondered how she should best reply, wishing her life wasn't so tangled in secrets. Audrey's earlier words echoed in Lily's head. *Truth will out. It always does.*

Chapter Four

Audrey tied a length of string round the bundle of parsley and dill that she'd plucked from the vegetable patch. Attaching the fragrant bunch to a nail banged into the wall above the kitchen sink, she rubbed the leaves between her fingers and breathed in their fresh scent. In times of rationing, herbs were a good way to add much-needed flavour and depth to a dish. She'd tried adding chives to the scones for the shop, and that had gone down well. Folk were grateful for any inventiveness.

'I hope there's enough to go round,' she muttered, turning to give the pot on the range a stir. Her appetite was whetted by the mouth-watering smell of the bacon rasher she'd chopped up into tiny pieces to include in the brown stew she was cooking. Being pregnant had benefits – apart from the obvious one of having a baby after years of believing she could never fall; there was the National Milk Scheme, which allowed extra milk for pregnant women, an extra egg allocation and an extra half-ration of meat a week. Not that she kept the extras for herself. No, that wouldn't do at all. She shared them with the bakery family. After all, everyone at the bakery would have to be involved with looking after the baby when it was born, so she could continue running the bakery business. Just thinking about how she would manage once the baby arrived made her head spin.

'Ouch!' she yelled, suddenly dropping the wooden spoon and doubling over in pain. Holding her hand against her abdomen, she limped over to a wooden chair at the kitchen table and carefully sat down, gently rubbing her bump. Frowning, she stared out of the kitchen window – where the sill was crowded with cucumber plants and a pot of red geraniums – at the early evening sky. A ridge of clouds half-obscured the setting sun and she wondered, for the umpteenth time, if she should tell the doctor about these pains she'd been having. No, there was only a matter of weeks to go until she was due and if she told the doctor he'd no doubt insist that she stop working, but she couldn't afford that. Nor did she want to be idle when there was always so much to do.

'Is something burning?' asked Elsie, Audrey's sister-in-law, who was living with her new husband William at the bakery, popping her head round the kitchen door. Audrey gasped and, now that the pain had subsided, leapt from her seat, picked up the spoon from the floor and dashed over to the range, where she quickly stirred the brown stew before it was ruined.

'Rescued it,' said Audrey. 'Goodness me, where's my head? Thank you, Elsie. How are you, love?'

Elsie came into the kitchen in her smart green uniform, stretched her arms above her head and yawned. Slim-built, with raven-black hair, Elsie usually had radiant skin but it looked bleached out, and her stance was one of someone who needed a good rest. She'd worked long hours as a clippie on the buses in Bournemouth since the war began and was now doing a bus driver training course too. Audrey was full of admiration for Elsie – she was a hard-working, big-hearted young woman, who'd been so understanding to William when he came back from the front line horrifically wounded in body and mind.

'Why don't you sit down, Audrey?' said Elsie. 'Put your feet up for once and let me cook today.'

'No, Elsie,' said Audrey. 'You've had a busy day and look like you need to rest. Why don't *you* sit down?'

Elsie grinned and gratefully sat down, resting back in the chair and turning her neck from side to side to ease out the cricks. Audrey poured her a cup of tea and placed it on the table. The last thing she wanted was to be treated like an invalid. Pregnant women through the ages had worked their socks off and still put a dinner on the table for a dozen mouths – without ever putting their feet up. She wasn't about to change that.

'Thank you,' said Elsie, holding the cup of tea in her hands and closing her eyes for a moment. 'I've looked forward to this cup of tea all day.'

'Did you hear about Jacques?' said Audrey. 'Would you believe the boy's alive? Lily received a telegram from him this morning. He was in a camp, but he managed to escape. That's all I know, but the most important thing is that he's alive. Miracles do happen.'

Elsie's eyes pinged open and a smile exploded onto her face.

'Oh my goodness, that's amazing news!' she said. 'His family must be over the moon!'

Audrey watched Elsie's glorious smile fade slightly as she moved her gaze to the window, and silently chastised herself. Other people's good news sometimes made people feel their own losses more strongly, she knew that. Elsie had her own hardships to bear. Her father, Alberto, was away in a prisoner-of-war camp himself on the Isle of Man. He had been arrested and escorted from his home in the middle of the night for being an Italian national, despite having been in England for over thirty years. Her mother Violet was in poor health and missed Alberto terribly, not to mention her young twin sisters, June and Joyce, who just wanted their papa home and couldn't understand why he was being treated in such a way by a country that was his home. Then there had been the dreadful loss of so many Italian internees on the torpedoed ship, the *Arandora Star* – a blight on the conscience of the government. It was a dreadful business.

And of course, Elsie's relationship with William hadn't been a smooth ride. He'd come back from France a different man in many ways, but she had stuck by him, continually loving and loyal.

'How are William's spirits at the moment?' Audrey asked, changing the subject. 'Do you think he's improved since your wedding?

He did seem to turn a corner at the end of last year, but I'm not daft, I know he's a tortured soul. Thank goodness he's got the bakehouse to keep him busy.'

Elsie smiled, a little sadly, and gave a small nod of her head. Audrey knew Elsie was holding something inside, but that she wasn't one to complain.

'What is it?' Audrey asked. 'Get it off your chest, Elsie. It's only me you're talking to. William might be my brother, but I'll make no judgements, whatever you say.'

Audrey got on with chopping up carrots – of which there was a nationwide glut – to give Elsie a chance to talk.

'Oh, it's just that every night William has a terrible nightmare,' Elsie said, wrapping her arms round her middle as if she had stomach cramp. 'He cries out and sits bolt upright, shivering and trembling, with his hands flying around as if he's trying to push his way out of a hole. He says he can't breathe, that he's buried. It's so dark in the room because of the blackout and it's as though he thinks he's suffocating.'

Audrey paused from chopping and turned to face Elsie, noticing her lips trembling as she spoke. Her heart went out to her sister-in-law. They had been married only six months earlier – almost certainly, nightmares were hardly the beginning to married life she'd hoped for.

'Gracious me,' said Audrey, remembering the dreadful secret that William had told her about in confidence before his wedding to Elsie. He had said he was going to put it all behind him, but clearly wasn't able to let it go. Men weren't keen on talking, but Audrey firmly believed that it helped – a problem shared was a problem halved.

'Has he ever explained what happened when he was fighting in France?' she ventured.

'You mean about the accident in the truck?' Elsie said, looking at her hands. 'Yes, it sounds dreadful – and to lose his foot must be so difficult to live with… he's often in pain, I know that.'

'I don't mean that,' Audrey said quietly. 'Has he mentioned anything else?'

'No,' said Elsie, frowning. 'He says he wants to put the whole experience in a box, lock it up and never open it again. Do you know something I don't?'

Audrey moved to the range and stirred her dish again, biting her lip. She didn't know whether to continue. Perhaps she'd said too much, but how was anything going to change between William and Elsie if he didn't open up to his wife?

'I may be speaking out of turn, but perhaps you should ask him to tell you everything,' Audrey said quietly. 'Ask him about his friend David.'

Elsie looked confused and opened her mouth to ask another question, but Audrey raised her wooden spoon to silence her.

'I've said all I should,' she said. 'Talk to William when you can. I'm sure it'll be for the best. Anyway, love, are you ready for our "make do and mend" sewing and clothes-swapping this evening? They'll all be here soon, and I've invited a new girl, Betty, who's trying out in the shop tomorrow as the new shop girl. I thought it would be a good way for us to get to know one another and I've some sewing needs doing. Renovations help the nation and all that.'

'Yes,' said Elsie quietly, clearly preoccupied by what Audrey had said about William. 'I've got some socks that need darning. I'm on fire-watching duty late tonight but I'll join you before then.'

'Good,' said Audrey, placing the lid on the brown stew and leaning her back against the kitchen counter. 'And don't worry, Elsie, things will get better.'

*

Elsie unbuttoned her green clippie jacket and hung it in the narrow solid-wood wardrobe, alongside William's Sunday best. She felt the soft material of his well-worn cotton shirt in her fingers, wondering what dreadful memory was plaguing his dreams and who David was. Glancing at the bed, she recalled the way his body had become drenched in sweat the previous night as he tossed and turned under the sheet as if he was literally wrestling his demons. None of the women she knew whose sons or husbands had returned from war too wounded to return to active service ever talked about a change in their menfolk's personalities. Was Elsie alone, or did other people just not speak of it, preferring to pretend nothing was wrong? Were they ashamed of what might be considered a moral weakness? She shook her head in dismay, wondering whether she should bring up what happened in France with William, as Audrey had suggested, or whether she should just stay quiet, as William obviously wished.

Moving to the window, she opened it wide and leaned on the sill, resting her chin in her hand, half-closing her eyes and savouring the warmth as the evening breeze caressed her skin. A sudden ripple of anxiety made her open her eyes and she blinked rapidly in the sinking sunshine: what if William's nightmares never went away? What if his mental scars ran more deeply and were as permanent as his facial scars? They were worse, really, she thought, for being invisible.

At that moment William burst through the door, wearing a big smile on his face. Surprised, Elsie immediately grinned back, her anxieties evaporating and spirits lifting. Perhaps she was worrying too much, but it was always so difficult to second-guess his mood.

'You look happy!' she said, kissing him quickly on the cheek before sitting on the bed and leaning her head back on the pillow.

'I've just been playing paper, scissors, stones with Mary in the bakehouse,' he said. 'She's such a sweet child – and brave considering all she's been through too. I could learn a thing or two from her.'

William was referring to the little evacuee girl who Audrey was in the process of adopting. Mary had tragically lost her brother, mother and father to the war and, when she had first arrived in Bournemouth, she hadn't said a single word for months; but despite all the grief she carried, bakery life agreed with her and she had come out of her shell.

'She is brave.' Elsie nodded in acknowledgment of Mary's courageous spirit. 'She's coped with more sorrow in her few years than some have in a whole lifetime.'

William, now sitting next to Elsie on the bed, pulled her into his body, wrapping his arms round her waist. With her head against his chest, she listened to the steady thump, thump of his heartbeat, relaxed into his body's warmth and closed her eyes.

'Makes me wonder if we should have a child of our own,' he said softly.

Elsie opened her eyes and blinked. She didn't reply straight away, but remained sitting with her head tucked under his chin, breathing in his scent – a combination of freshly baked bread and flour – and listening to his heartbeat. She felt a myriad of emotions as she gently moved from her position, reached for his hands and looked him directly in the eye. Deep down, she felt that William was in no fit state to become a father. Besides, Elsie was determined to volunteer her services for the war effort and was committed to doing her bit. With the men away, she was needed on the buses and felt she was helping the war to conclude faster. She wanted it over as quickly as possible, for her father Alberto to be returned from the Isle of Man – and for life with William to feel on a more even keel before they started a family. Cupping his face with her hands, she smiled and slowly shook her head.

'I don't think it's the right time to have a child,' she said gently. 'You'll be needed even more in the bakehouse, at all hours, with Audrey about to have her baby. And if I'm not working on the buses, who will be?'

'The government are encouraging civilians to have babies,' said William. 'They're saying it's a duty to our country to bring more babies into the world. It's one in the eye for Hitler, isn't it?'

Elsie couldn't hide her shock and irritation.

'Why, because a baby would replace a man who's been killed? To provide more soldiers to send off to fight?' said Elsie. 'Isn't that demeaning the lives of those we've lost? In my opinion avenging Hitler isn't a reason to have a family. No, William, I'd rather do my bit to help win this war by doing war work and volunteering, then think of having children later, when peacetime comes. There'll be time for a family after the war, I know it.'

With a deep, exasperated sigh, William stood up from the bed, yanked open a drawer from the chest of drawers and pulled out a fresh vest ready for his next stint in the bakehouse. His smile had vanished, and Elsie felt guilty for crushing his enthusiasm and high spirits. She wanted to boost his happiness, not quash it, and she chastised herself for not handling the situation better. But at the same time, another voice in her head told her that she had to be honest about her feelings and couldn't keep treading on eggshells around him. Otherwise, how would their marriage ever work?

'Anyway, did you hear the news about Jacques, the French soldier who stayed at the bakery?' babbled Elsie, knowing that this news would cheer him. 'He's written to Lily to say he's alive! Course she's worried about telling him about Joy. But isn't it good news?! His mother must be celebrating, mustn't she?'

The atmosphere in the room grew suddenly colder and William seemed to withdraw into himself, completely, as if he'd pulled up a drawbridge and locked it shut. Having finished dressing, he gave her a quick smile and a nod but said nothing.

'Aren't you pleased to hear that?' Elsie said, confused. 'I mean, don't we need news like that, to give us all hope? To lift us?'

Looking agitated, he rubbed his forehead and slowly lifted his head to face her.

'Yes,' he snapped, 'of course I'm glad to hear it. I just can't help thinking of the other families who don't get good news. Those families whose lives fall apart when the messenger boy knocks on their door and hands them a telegram from the War Office. Can you imagine how that must be for those poor mothers? Not knowing how their sons died, only imagining the pain they suffered, knowing that they were probably alone and in agony… it's, well, to be honest, Elsie, just thinking about it fills me with rage.'

William pressed his hands against both sides of his head, as if it was about to burst with pressure. Elsie frowned, her stomach somersaulting and heart pounding. His anger was tangible and made her shiver.

'William?' she said, approaching him and resting her hand on his arm, but he brushed off her affection, snatched his crutches from where they leaned on the wall and headed towards the door.

'William, why won't you talk to me?' she said as he limped out of the bedroom and let the door swing shut. Reducing her voice to a whisper, she continued: 'Why haven't you told me who David is?'

By now William was downstairs. With a grunt of frustration, Elsie picked up his shirt and threw it at the door, where it fell limply into a crumpled heap. She lay down on the bed, thudding the back of her head on the pillow and kicking her heels into the mattress as she stared up at the ceiling. She released a furious sigh. He *has* to talk to me, she decided. I'll *make* him talk to me, even if it's the last thing I do.

Chapter Five

Later that evening, after the family had enjoyed stew and fresh vegetables, Audrey brought out a sweet treat.

'I've made my honey cake,' she said, easing herself carefully into the empty chair at the kitchen table. Heavily pregnant as she was, everything took a little bit more effort than it used to. 'There's no eggs or butter in it, but it's sweet,' she continued, placing the fragrant cake in the middle of the table. 'It'll have to do until we can get all our favourites back.'

Audrey smiled at the assembled group, whose eyes were fixed on the cake in front of them. Outside the window the evening sky glowed with the orange embers of the setting sun, just visible above the sea on the horizon, giving the kitchen a warm, golden glow – as if the whole room were bathed in honey. The wireless played out in the background; Gracie Fields was singing, and just for the briefest moment, in spite of all the all-pervading and ever-present worry about the menfolk away at war, Audrey felt a brief sense of peace. Jacques was safe – that was such marvellous news – and she was so excited to be expecting a baby. Even in wartime, there *were* reasons to be cheerful.

Sweeping her hand over the worn wooden tabletop, which had survived last year's blast when a bomb hit the front of the bakery, she lifted the large brown teapot and served Elsie, Pat, little Mary, Lily and Lily's friend Christine a cup of tea, then gently removed the delicate beaded crochet cover from the top of the milk jug.

'Help yourselves to the milk,' she said. 'Being pregnant, I get extra on the National Milk Scheme, so don't feel you need to be frugal.'

The women murmured in appreciation as Audrey cut the dense, sticky cake and passed round generous slices. Living in austerity meant that every treat was fully savoured. That was one thing about this dreadful war – it made you appreciate everything you had, whether it be family, a roof over your head, a night without an air raid siren going off or the ingredients to put together a decent dinner.

'Oh, what would we do without you and your ingenious cakes to help us through these dark times?' said Pat, still proudly wearing her WVS smock and peering at Audrey with bright blue eyes the spit of Charlie's but magnified through her round spectacles. 'Now sweets are on the ration I've heard people are chopping each sweet into four pieces, to make them last. Or, for those lucky enough to get their hands on a Mars Bar, they're slicing them into seven pieces, so they can have a slice every day. It's amazing what folk will do to cheer up their days. Oh, but I must tell you this: I was in a queue today and one woman, well, I've never heard so much complaining because the shopkeeper wouldn't sell her one single shoe. She didn't want to spend her clothing coupons on a whole pair, so insisted on buying just one single shoe! What's that shopkeeper going to do with the other one? You'd think she would just be sensible, button her lip and get on with it, but no, she argued until she was blue in the face!'

Pat raised her eyebrows so high in disgust they almost touched her hairline. Lily caught Audrey's eye and Audrey laughed affectionately. Her mother-in-law was a tough old boot, intensely patriotic and remarkably hard-working. She threw herself into any WVS task without a word of complaint, whether it be helping to coordinate housing for people made homeless following raids, collecting books for servicemen and women or grooming dogs for their hair, which was spun into yarn and knitted like wool.

'I expect you set her straight!' said Audrey, smiling at Pat, who nodded enthusiastically.

'One shoe indeed!' Pat tutted.

'This is delicious, Mrs Barton,' said Lily's friend Christine, the young woman who was staying at the convalescent home after coming to Bournemouth from Bristol with her baby for some respite after the horrific Bristol Blitz bombing. 'The food in the home isn't very good – but their teacakes are tasty.'

'That's because we supply them with their bread and teacakes! Every morning at 7 a.m., our delivery boy drops them to the door,' Audrey replied, giving her another slice of cake. 'How's that little girl of yours doing? Bless her heart!'

Christine's daughter, Aggi, was slowly being exposed to the sound of aircraft to help her change her negative associations of the noise.

'She's much improved,' said Christine. 'I think we'll return to Bristol soon, otherwise my friends and family – or what's left of them – will forget us!'

Lily draped her arm round Christine and briefly rested her head on her new friend's shoulder.

'We'll miss you!' she said, but Christine playfully pushed her away.

'You've got Jacques to think about now, Lily!' she said. 'Your handsome French sweetheart!'

Audrey smiled as Lily blushed, but didn't miss the look of apprehension that passed over Lily's face. She made a mental note to talk to her about it all when they were alone together – a sweetheart coming back from the dead was a lot to cope with. Noticing the time on the clock, Audrey set out another plate and cleared her throat.

'So, I'm expecting Betty any moment – she's a little late,' said Audrey. 'I'm giving her a trial in the shop, to see if she can do Maggie's old job, and I asked her to come along tonight for a slice of cake and to meet you all. I've said we're having a clothes exchange and a sewing, darning or knitting get-together, so I hope you will welcome her.'

At that moment there was a knock on the door and Audrey pulled her apron off and smoothed down her dress, which was an old raspberry pink frock that she'd sewn contrasting floral front panels into to allow space for her bump. She was entitled to extra clothing coupons for maternity wear but had decided to do the right thing and get by with what she already had. Where she could make savings to help the war effort, she would.

'Budge up, Mary dear,' said Audrey over her shoulder. 'Make room for Betty. I'll go and fetch her.'

Opening the door to Betty and welcoming her in, Audrey was once again struck by the girl's threadbare dress and uneven haircut. Frowning slightly, she wondered how she could possibly mention it without offending her – she didn't want one of the older customers to get in there first and hurt her feelings. Some of the ladies had tongues sharp as knives.

'Come upstairs, Betty,' she said. 'We're all in the kitchen, tucking into that honey cake I told you about.'

Opening the kitchen door, Audrey introduced Betty to the women and Mary, who all greeted her with smiles. Pat, standing to shake the girl's hand, patted her on the head.

'I'm Pat, Audrey's mother-in-law,' she said. 'I see you've cut your own hair, lovey? I think that needs straightening up. I know, I know, there's no time for going to the hairdresser's in wartime and it feels like too much of an indulgence, doesn't it, but I'm as good as any hairdresser. Let me get my scissors.'

Audrey, blushing on Betty's account, murmured in protest, 'Well, I…' but Pat was insistent.

'Sit down, Betty,' she instructed.

'I… I…' said Betty, her pink cheeks turning scarlet.

'It won't take me a minute,' said Pat, gently pushing down on Betty's shoulders so she sat down on a chair. 'This is Elsie, Audrey's sister-in-law. That's Lily, Audrey's stepsister. This is Mary, who came to us as an evacuee but is now one of the family, aren't you, Mary?

Then this is Christine, who's Lily's friend. She's here from Bristol; the local convalescent home offered respite to mothers with babies who had suffered during the Bristol Blitz, poor mites.'

Audrey watched Betty turn even redder as she nodded and smiled at the group. The poor girl seemed desperately shy, Audrey thought, and the last thing she needed was Pat cutting her hair in front of an audience. There was no telling Pat though; she was a force to be reckoned with. Audrey would have to think about a way to give Betty a new dress without embarrassing her further – some folk were very proud about that kind of thing.

'Pat, maybe this isn't the…' started Audrey, but Pat was already snipping at Betty's hair. Audrey smiled apologetically at the young woman. She set out a slice of cake for her and placed a cup of tea in her hand. Betty mouthed a 'thank you' and carefully sipped her tea.

'There,' said Pat after a couple of minutes. 'You're all straight now. When you're working front of house in the bakery you have to look the part. Our older customers are very fussy about appearances. Why don't you tell us all about yourself. Where are you from?'

Betty felt the bottom of her newly clipped hair and after a strained 'thank you', sat with everyone at the table. She had her back half-turned to Christine, who was chewing the inside of her cheek and narrowing her eyes, as if she was trying to remember something.

'I'm staying in a rented room in Lansdowne, but I'm here from Portsmouth—' started Betty, but Christine interrupted.

'I thought you were going to say you're from Bristol, like me,' said Christine. 'I could swear I recognise you from somewhere. Maybe the tobacco factory? Have you ever worked there?'

'No,' Betty said vehemently, shaking her head. 'Never heard of it.'

'Oh,' said Christine coldly. 'That's odd.'

Audrey felt the atmosphere in the room change, as if an icy wind was blowing in from the sea. She moved over to the window and slammed it shut. A sudden silence fell over the room and, detecting

Betty's discomfort, Audrey felt confused. Something was going on between those girls but she didn't know what. Lifting down her sewing basket from the dresser, she coughed to gain everyone's attention.

'Shall we begin knitting and darning?' she asked. 'Betty, you can work on this bakery smock, so you've something to wear when you come in tomorrow. It used to belong to Maggie. It needs a small patch here to strengthen the elbow, that's all. I'm going to try to drop the waist on Mary's school dress here, to keep pace with her growing!'

Audrey patted Mary's head and kissed her cheek, quietly delighted that Mary was growing like a weed and flourishing in her care. All those hours spent digging in the allotment and those spoons of rosehip syrup had put roses in Mary's cheeks. She was going to be a lovely older sister to the baby when he or she was born too.

'Remember, ladies, in these times no economy is too small,' said Pat.

Elsie laughed affectionately.

'You sound like those announcements on the radio from the Board of Trade,' said Elsie, then, sitting straighter and speaking in an upper-class accent: 'Every woman is her own clothes doctor!'

Everyone laughed, then they all started to pick up needles and threads and the project they were sewing, while Christine sat still as the stocks, staring at Betty in confusion.

'I just know I recognise you from somewhere,' she muttered, frowning. 'I can't work it out. It's giving me the heebie-jeebies!'

But Betty just smiled and shrugged as if she didn't know what Christine was talking about and, with her head down so her hair fell over her face, started sewing the bakery overall until Christine lost interest. Only Audrey noticed that Betty's hands were trembling as she began to stitch. Briefly resting her hand on Betty's shoulder, she smiled at her.

'There's no rush,' she said kindly. 'Take your time, love. Oh, and I've got a couple of dresses that might fit you if you'd be so kind as to take them off my hands? They're no good for me anymore, but I think they'd be lovely on you, with a little nip and tuck. I'll just fetch them from upstairs. They're wasted hanging in the wardrobe and never seeing the light of day.'

'You need to slow down, young lady,' said Pat, gently grabbing Audrey's wrist. 'You've not stopped since we got here. Let me or Mary get the dresses for you.'

Audrey tutted, waved her hand in the air dismissively and went up to her bedroom. In the quiet of her room, which smelled faintly of her Pond's face cream and of the cologne that Charlie used to wear on special occasions, she let her gaze rest on the framed photograph of her and Charlie on their wedding day. From nowhere, her eyes filled with tears, and she wiped at them in frustration. She missed Charlie dreadfully and it pained her that he hadn't even acknowledged the letter that she'd sent to tell him she was pregnant. What if he didn't know she was with child? What if all he ever was to this baby was a photograph? How she yearned to talk to him, to hear his firm but gentle voice, to feel the warmth of his arms round her…

'Oh, stop it, you daft thing,' she told herself. You could be in a constant state of bad nerves if you didn't control yourself.

Opening the wardrobe door, she pulled out two day dresses that she thought would fit Betty. They weren't anything special, but something gave her the feeling that the girl probably only owned the dress she stood up in, so these would do her a good turn. Draping them over her arm, Audrey stopped suddenly as a sharp pain dug into her abdomen and lower back. Her face paled with the pain as she bent over and pressed her fingers into her lower stomach. Hobbling to the edge of the bed, she rested for a moment on the mattress until the pain subsided. Stricken with panic, she hoped to goodness that the baby was safe and healthy. What if she really was doing too much? Pat's words repeated in her head: *You need to slow down, young lady.*

*

Betty didn't fully breathe again that evening until she was back in her rented digs, having raced up the communal wooden staircase and slammed shut the door to her tiny, dank bedroom on the second floor of the shabby hotel that had seen better days. She leaned against the door and locked it. Her heart pounded in her chest and goose-bumps erupted on her arms as Christine's words echoed in her head.

I just know I recognise you from somewhere. Of course she *did* recognise her from Bristol. Christine's husband, Dick, was a friend of Robert's – they'd gone drinking together before the war. Betty knew that Christine would quickly cotton on to her lie, probably already had. She wondered if she should try to tell Christine the truth about Robert? Perhaps she would understand… or would she still tell Dick, and then Dick would tell Robert where Betty had gone. Oh dear, it was all such a mess!

'I should never have gone there this evening,' she admonished herself aloud. She almost hadn't, but the promise of a homely evening with Audrey and her family had been too tempting to forgo. With shaking hands, she draped the dresses Audrey had kindly given her over the back of a chair and moved over to the narrow bed, kicking off her shoes and quickly undressing to her slip before climbing under the thin eiderdown. Shivering, she rested her head on the envelope-thin pillow, blinking in the darkness, trying to work out what she should do for the best. Somewhere in the distance came the sound of aircraft, and Betty held her breath for a moment, dreading the wail of the air raid siren. Trying to keep calm, she reminded herself that there was a shared shelter in the basement of the hotel so she didn't have far to go to safety. When the siren didn't sound and the sound of aircraft faded, she sighed in relief, forcing the terrifying memories of the Bristol Blitz from her mind.

Tossing and turning in bed, Betty couldn't stop worrying about Christine. If she hadn't already, how long would it be before she remembered who Betty was? Perhaps she shouldn't even turn up to the job at the bakery tomorrow. Perhaps she should move on to another town instead and disappear again. But she'd already paid a non-refundable month's rent up front on this room, and she wouldn't want to let Audrey down after all she'd done for her. No, she thought, trying to get comfortable in the bed, which squeaked and creaked when she moved, she would either have to speak to Christine and tell her the truth about why she'd run away, or avoid her at all costs and hope that she forgot all about Betty.

Just as she was beginning to drift off to sleep, she was disturbed by a heated discussion, followed by laughter, between a man and woman in the room next to hers. Instantly, her thoughts went to Robert and Doris. Thinking of them together, clinched in an embrace, her heart ached, and she pulled her bony knees up to her chest, hugging them tight. She felt so utterly betrayed by Robert, who she had loved so much; and now, even in Bournemouth, his wrongdoing was still affecting her life. What made it all the more terrible was how silly she felt for not having known that he was married to another woman and a father to three young children. Was she really stupid and short-sighted enough to have missed the signs? Of course, now that she knew the truth, when she looked back she saw signs everywhere – the nights he was away with no explanation, the lack of money, the exhaustion and irritability…

'What a fool I am to have trusted him!' she said out loud into the empty room, shocked by the fury in her own voice.

At least I have his savings, she thought bitterly, but that fact did little to cheer her up. Besides, his savings wouldn't last long. As she slipped into a blank, dreamless sleep, she made a vow to herself: I will never trust a man ever again. Not ever.

Chapter Six

With Joy fast asleep in her small bed, Lily tried, for the fourth night since he had written, to write a reply to Jacques. With the blackout blind down and just a flickering oil lamp for light, her eyes were watering with strain and tiredness as she tried to find the right words, but she felt she must reply to him before another day passed.

It was almost midnight and though she could hear Uncle John working in the bakehouse, preparing the dough for tomorrow's bread, she suspected the rest of the bakery was asleep. Tomorrow she would be at the library early, helping to teach a group of refugees to speak English. Tonight was the only opportunity she had to reply to Jacques, but her mind was blank. There was so much to say – too much. After thinking Jacques was dead for over a year, how could she convey the joy she felt on hearing he was alive in just a few words? And how did she confess to him that when they'd met she'd been pregnant, after having an affair with a married man – a socially unacceptable sin other girls had been locked up for in the mental asylum. Lily shivered, counting her blessings that Audrey had taken her in and been so understanding. But would Jacques be as understanding?

Maybe I should make up something more palatable, she thought, before quickly dismissing the idea. It would have to be the truth, or nothing – but perhaps she could buy herself some time.

Sighing deeply, she tried again, this time writing a brief message to say how delighted she was to receive his news. *I have a great deal to tell you,* she wrote, *but it can wait.* Signing off and quickly folding up the letter, she tucked it into her book, feeling disappointed in herself. Preparing to blow out the oil lamp and get some sleep, she stopped when there was a gentle knock on the door. She tiptoed across the room and opened it to find Elsie standing there in her long cream nightdress, her hair falling over her shoulders in long black tendrils.

'I can't sleep,' she whispered. 'Can I come in?'

Lily welcomed her in and both girls sat on the bed, covering their toes with the blanket. Before Elsie had married William, the girls had shared a bedroom and spent many a night talking into the early hours.

'I can't tell Jacques about Joy just yet,' Lily admitted. 'I can't blurt out everything in the first letter I send. He says he's thought about me every day since we met. I'm scared to burst his bubble.'

Elsie smiled in understanding and nodded. 'How do you feel about him? Have you thought about him too?'

'Yes,' said Lily. 'But I thought he was dead, so I deliberately tried *not* to think about him. Remember that drawing he did of me? I still have it. I'm worried because what if he expects more from me? I suspect he thinks he wants us to be together, one day, but he doesn't know about Joy and well, even if he did accept her, which he won't, I don't know if I want to be married to anyone.'

'Married?' said Elsie with a smile, nudging Lily gently with her elbow. 'Aren't you getting ahead of things there? He's only written to you to tell you he's still alive – don't worry, he's not proposing marriage just yet!'

'I know, I know, but remember the love letter he wrote after we first met?' Lily said. 'I think he's built me up into someone I'm not. I don't think I'd make anyone a good wife. I don't think marriage is for me.'

'Why?' asked Elsie. 'Have I put you off?'

'No.' Lily laughed. 'It's more that I have other plans for Joy and me. I want to be independent and able to provide for Joy myself. I want to have the freedom to work and show her that women don't have to take the conventional road in life. I don't see myself as a wife, scrubbing doorsteps and ironing collars. I don't want that for Joy either.'

Elsie chuckled, leaned her head against the wall and yawned.

'I don't think scrubbing steps is what being a wife is about any more, not in wartime,' she said. 'It's about being a friend. It's about trying to understand what your husband has endured if they've been in battle and supporting them through it all. That's what I think, anyway. Not that I'm doing very well on that front, I have to admit.'

Elsie rubbed her face with her palms and sighed.

'What's wrong?' said Lily. 'You've been awfully quiet lately. Is there a problem you'd like to talk about?'

Elsie shrugged and sighed. 'Oh, I… yes, it's William,' she said. 'Sometimes, I can't seem to reach him. I thought he was feeling better, but he's not, and he won't tell me what's troubling him, despite me asking. Sometimes he won't get out of bed or even speak to me. He was once so full of life.'

Lily smiled sadly at her friend, who she could see was desperately troubled, but she had little advice. She thought about her own father, Victor, who, after losing his wife – Lily's mother – had completely shut down, as if he'd closed his emotions off like a tap. There had been no way to reach him either.

'I think some men don't like to dwell and they need to be left to get on with it, perhaps?' said Lily. 'Audrey said that when Charlie came home on leave that time, he didn't want to talk about what he'd seen on the front line at all. Like it was all a bad dream that he could leave behind him.'

Elsie nodded, but her eyes misted over. 'I understand that,' she said. 'But William's bad dreams are spilling over into his days. They've caught up with him and are making him unhappy and I don't know what to do to help him.'

Lily reached for her friend's hand and gave it a gentle squeeze. 'You said it yourself,' she said. 'Be his friend.'

*

Elsie crept back into her bedroom, trying not to disturb William. He would have to get up soon to join John in the bakehouse but was having a few hours of sleep while he could. Their bedroom, the attic room, was always warm and cosy, being at the top of the bakery – even the floorboards were warm underfoot – and it smelled faintly of the apples that Audrey had kept in the room in crates to dry out over the winter. She tiptoed across the dark room, the warm boards creaking as she moved, and lifted up the sheet to climb in next to her husband. In the darkness, she gently brushed her fingers across his scarred face.

'Darling William,' she whispered as she lay down next to him and rested her head on the pillow and her hand on his chest. Trying to empty her head of her worries, she closed her eyes and was allowing her tired body to relax when—

'GET OFF ME!' William bellowed at the top of his lungs, sitting bolt upright in bed and forcefully shoving Elsie off. 'GET AWAY FROM ME! LET ME OUT! I CAN'T BREATHE!'

'William!' cried Elsie, half-crying and with her heart racing as she landed in a tangle of sheets on the floor, banging her arm and hip on the side of the bed. 'William, stop!'

'GET AWAY!' he continued to shout. 'I CAN'T SEE! I CAN'T BREATHE! I'M SUFFOCATING!'

Because of the blackout the room was pitch-black, and, her hands groping desperately in the darkness for the top of the bedside table where she kept her small hand torch, she quickly clicked it on, turning its glow towards William. Violently shaking and clutching the edge of the sheet in his hands, her handsome, lovely husband looked like a feral animal, glistening with sweat and with tears running from wild eyes and down his cheeks. On his face, for a split second, she saw darkness and death and red skies and violence and pure terror. It was an awful sight and it took her breath away. What depths of human depravity had he witnessed? Shaking her head in a mixture of pity and fear, she turned the torchlight away from him, sat on the mattress beside him and grabbed hold of his hand. He was panting now, as if he'd just run ten miles. Gently rubbing the top of his hand, she made soothing noises until he seemed calmer.

'William?' she said quietly when he was finally calm. 'Are you awake now?'

He nodded, looking ashamed. His shoulders were hunched and his knees drawn up to his chin.

'It's my heart,' he whimpered. 'It's racing. It's not feeling right.'

Elsie gulped, determined not to cry. It was a test of her will, but she had to remain strong for both of them. Though she felt like curling up into a ball herself, William had nothing to offer in the way of comfort right now, she knew.

'You had a nightmare,' she said, trying to control the tremor in her voice. 'You've had so many nightmares. Can you tell me why?'

Running his hands through his hair, William sighed deeply as if preparing to speak, but then the air raid siren began its haunting call, interrupting the delicate moment. Instead he just blinked, now fully awake and collecting himself together.

'You'd better get to the shelter with the others,' he said. 'I'll go to the bakehouse to help John and keep an eye on the ovens. We can use the baking table for cover if we need to. Come on, there's no time to lose.'

The moment was lost. Elsie felt the fight drain out of her. Quickly, she pulled on her coat over her nightdress and pushed her feet into her shoes, forcing herself to focus on preparing to go down to the Anderson shelter in the backyard. She knew that William had been about to talk to her about what was tormenting him and was desperate to hear what he had to say, but for now, she said nothing more. As William grabbed his crutches and before they parted on the stairs, Elsie quickly kissed his cheek and squeezed his hand. 'I will help you,' she said bravely, and he gave her a small, sad smile before disappearing into the heart of the bakery to help ensure the bread was ready for the next day.

Elsie met Audrey, Mary and Lily with Joy in her arms at the bottom of the stairs and the women hurried out into the backyard, where the Anderson shelter, topped with soil where they were growing leeks and onions, was lit by the moon. Just before closing the door behind them, with the rattle of gunfire in the distance, Elsie saw a red glow in the sky along the coast to the east. Her heart sank. The war was unrelenting.

'Looks like Southampton's getting it,' she said quietly, fastening the door behind them and perching on the bench, staring down at her shoes. Mary and Joy lay in the little bunk Charlie had made and immediately fell back to sleep, while the women huddled up on the bench, covering their legs with a blanket.

'At least it's dry now,' said Audrey, referring to the damp nights they'd endured earlier in the year when, because of heavy rain, many Anderson shelters had flooded. 'Are you all right, Elsie love? You look pale.'

Elsie rubbed her eyes and nodded.

'I've decided I'm going to ask William to tell me everything,' she said. 'Something is tormenting him, something bad. I need to know the truth.'

Audrey squeezed her hand. 'All I can say is that it's complicated, but that he thought he was doing the right thing,' she muttered, her face clouding over. 'He thinks he failed, but as someone clever once said – and I remind myself of this often – there is only one failure in life possible, and that is not to be true to the best one knows.'

Elsie smiled, leaned her head on Audrey's shoulder and closed her eyes, listening to the terrifying sounds of war playing out overhead.

Chapter Seven

Two weeks after her first trial day at the bakery, Betty was officially the new shop girl and was beginning to find her feet at Barton's, learning her penny buns from her teacakes and her fresh scones from her stales. The customers had welcomed her with open arms, many of them seeming to relish the opportunity to talk to a new person about their family goings-on. It was funny how, as a shop girl, you were privy to so much personal information – Audrey said that one of the most important things to remember was to give every customer your personal attention, to offer a bright smile and a warm shoulder and never judge a person, whatever they said, until you'd walked a mile in their shoes. This came naturally to Betty and she rather enjoyed finding out about people's lives – a little selfishly, perhaps, because their stories of heartache or suffering made her feel less awful about her own embarrassing situation.

Every morning, on her way to catch the bus from her room in Lansdowne to the bakery in Southbourne, Betty walked past the tall, grand Metropole Hotel, where hundreds of Canadian airmen were billeted. Often there would be a group of uniformed men smoking outside the hotel, preparing to go out on their morning drill. She tried not to, but she knew that when she passed one airman in particular – a young man with a warm smile, a shock of white-blond hair and dark brown eyes – she walked a little taller and held her chin a little higher. This morning was no different.

'Morning, beautiful girl,' the blond airman said in his alluring Canadian accent. Unable to stop a smile creeping onto her lips, Betty silently reprimanded herself.

You're still a married woman, for goodness' sake, she thought, trying not to blush.

'Can I walk with you?' he said boldly and walked alongside her for a few steps, keeping in time with her pace, so close that their sleeves brushed. Without slowing down, she turned and looked at him, realising that, up close, he was even more handsome than she'd thought.

'Those red lips and pink roses on your cheeks can't be real, can they?' he said in mock horror. 'You must be wearing some blush,' he added with a cheeky smile, to which she raised her eyebrows and rolled her eyes. She wasn't – and he knew as much.

'I'm Sam, by the way,' he said. 'What's your name?'

She didn't reply, so he pushed her. 'Go on, tell me, what's your name?' He laughed. 'Or is it a national secret?'

Seeing her bus pulling up at the stop, she increased her pace, leaving him behind on the pavement, but not before finally muttering; 'Betty. I'm Betty,' and giving him a little smile that she couldn't suppress, despite knowing better.

'Good to meet you, beautiful Betty!' he hollered after her in the street, which made her cheeks burn. She wasn't used to compliments and couldn't remember the last time she'd had one. 'Maybe we could meet up some time?' he shouted, running his hand through his hair and grinning.

Hastily stepping onto the bus and knowing that he was still standing in the street as it pulled off, she tried not to look back at him, but just as the bus was about to swing round the corner and disappear out of view, she couldn't resist glancing back. He was still standing there, his hands pushed into his pockets, a big grin on his face. He raised his hand and she waved a little wave in return – such a simple action, but it suddenly felt too intimate.

'Gracious,' she whispered, holding her cool fingers against her hot cheeks. She flicked her eyes around the faces of the people on the bus, but nobody seemed to have noticed that she was burning with a combination of shock, pride and embarrassment, thank goodness. Sinking into a seat, she folded her hands on her lap and tried to calm down her frantic thoughts.

Perhaps I shouldn't have told him my name, she thought. *What was I thinking?*

They could never be friends. For one, she was married and secondly, the fewer people she knew in this new life she was forging, the safer she was. Since arriving in Bournemouth she'd managed so far to avoid too many questions about herself, apart from when Christine had recognised her, of course. The customers were satisfied with her first name and only really wanted to tell her their news and, thankfully, Betty hadn't seen Christine again since that first night. She hoped the girl had forgotten all about her. Secretly, she found the thought of Sam quite thrilling, but she knew she should avoid him. Men were not to be trusted, she knew that only too well. Why would he be any different?

Thinking of untrustworthy men and staring out of the bus window, her thoughts turned to Robert. She wondered how he was coping without her, and realised with a sinking heart that he might actually be pleased that she'd disappeared without a trace. Perhaps she'd made life simpler for him. Now he could focus on Doris and his kiddies, without the obligation of being married to Betty. Perhaps everyone in Bristol thought she'd died in an air raid – people did disappear. Shaking her head in dismay, she felt a rush of anger towards him. 'I'm better off without you, Robert Mitchell,' she muttered, then realised she was at her stop and jumped up from her seat, ready to disembark.

Arriving at the bakery, where the delicious aroma of warm bread drifted into the street and the sing-song voice of Audrey chatting to Mary lifted her spirits, Betty put all thoughts of Robert and Sam firmly from her mind. The bakery was her life now, her rented room her home.

'Morning!' she called to Audrey, who, helped by Mary, was polishing the shop window where BAKERY was written in elegant gold lettering. Despite being pregnant, Audrey never rested – the woman was a workhorse!

'Morning, love,' said Audrey, smiling at her. 'There's a pot of tea and a warm bun in the kitchen if you want a bit of breakfast before you start. You're looking lovely today! The Bournemouth sea air must be doing you good. Beautiful day, isn't it?'

'Yes, it's going to be a warm one, I think,' said Betty, smiling appreciatively at the bright blue sky. She felt great warmth for Audrey, who had welcomed her into the bakery without interrogating her about her past and whose cheerful manner was good for the whole community's morale. Inside the shop, Betty put on her bakery overall and quickly helped to put the baskets of fresh buns and loaves in the window. She realised, as she handled the hot bread, that she loved her new job.

'I'll make this new life work, no matter what,' she told herself, preparing to serve the first few customers, women who shopped early so they could still get to their war jobs in factories on time.

Mid-morning, when the queue had died down, Pat arrived with a WVS overall for Betty. Handing it over the counter, she regaled her with the numerous WVS jobs that needed doing, and Betty felt pleased for the opportunity to become more involved and be more helpful. The busier she was, the less time she had for agonising over Robert – or dreaming about Sam.

'When you're done in the bakery this afternoon there's an important job that needs doing,' said Pat, resting for a moment in the bakery chair. 'It's the Bournemouth book scheme. We're collecting unwanted books and magazines for the waste paper drive, but we're also taking books to the military personnel billeted here, to give them something to do in their hours off. Keep all those young men out of trouble! Can you help me distribute them to some of the hotels that the men and women are staying at? I've had so many donations, I can't possibly do it alone.'

'I'd be happy to help, Pat,' Betty agreed, smiling. But on seeing Lily and Christine enter the bakery, her smile faded and she froze. 'Oh, I just need to go outside for a moment. Excuse me…'

Betty rushed past a confused-looking Pat, Lily and Christine out into the street. Not knowing what to do, she started to cross the road and headed towards the post office. Christine called after her.

'Betty!' she yelled. 'Come back here, will you? I've a question for you. It's important.'

Betty wished she could run away up the street, but knowing Pat and Lily's eyes were also on her, she couldn't. Sighing, she returned slowly to where Christine was standing outside the bakery, making a performance of lighting up a cigarette. Just from the expression on her face, Betty knew her cover was blown and that Christine was going to take great pleasure in telling her as much.

'I know who you are, Betty Mitchell,' Christine said, blowing smoke in her face. 'You're my husband Dick's friend, Robert Mitchell's wife, aren't you? Have you done a runner from Bristol? I'm going back there today. Just called in to say farewell.'

Betty folded her arms across her chest and chewed the inside of her cheek.

'Don't say anything to anyone in Bristol, will you?' she said. 'Don't say you've seen me. Please don't tell Robert. I had to get away. It was… difficult.'

'Why?' Christine pushed, her interest piqued. 'What are you hiding? My Dick has a lot of time for Robert, thinks he's a fine, hard-working sort. I'm sure he'll be interested to hear that I've seen you.'

Betty blanched. People in Bristol did think Robert was a good man. If only they knew the truth. Betty could quickly set Christine straight, but something stopped her from bad-mouthing her husband. Was it loyalty to him, or embarrassment on her own part?

'I'm not hiding anything,' Betty said, feeling irritated. 'I just don't want him to know where I am. It's complicated and I don't want to go into it really.'

'Does he beat you?' said Christine, her eyes open wide. 'Cos if he does, then I'll let him know what I think of him.'

'No,' said Betty, sighing. 'It's not that. He's never hurt me.'

'Then what is it?' she said. 'Have you got another fella or something? Have you done the dirty on him?'

'No!' said Betty, feeling increasingly annoyed by Christine's nosiness. 'Why are you so interested? It's nothing to do with you! Can't you just forget you saw me?'

Christine glared at her and Betty returned the glare. What if she told Christine the truth and she reported Robert to the police? Even though he had treated her so badly, she didn't wish that on him.

'I'm just wondering why you're lying to these good people at the bakery,' said Christine. 'That's what it's got to do with me. They've done nothing but show you kindness and you're not telling them the truth. You told them you're called Smith and that you're from Portsmouth, so what are you hiding?'

'I needed some time to think,' said Betty, her heart pounding. 'Why don't you just leave me alone to get on with my own life?'

But Christine wouldn't leave it alone. In fact, the more Betty insisted, the more interested she became.

'What's it worth then, your secret?' she said, changing tack. She glanced through the bakery window and gave Lily, Pat and Audrey an innocent little wave before moving closer to Betty. 'It must be something pretty big if you've run all the way to Bournemouth and you're lying to Audrey Barton, who has a heart of gold.' She paused and narrowed her eyes, as if devising a plan. 'You can buy my silence,' she continued, 'but I'm expensive. Half your bakery wage or I'll go down the docks today and tell Robert what I know.'

Betty pushed Christine away from her. Christine shoved her back, hard. Suddenly enraged, Betty shoved the other woman up against the wall.

'I'm not paying you a penny,' Betty said. 'That's blackmail.'

She got as close to her face as she dared, desperately trying to intimidate her, but Christine just laughed a bitter laugh.

'Liar!' said Christine. 'Fake!'

'Shut up!' Betty said, holding on to her wrist. 'You're a bitch! Why do you even care about my life? Just do me a favour and shove off!'

Suddenly there was a hand on Betty's shoulder, and she spun round on her heel to see Audrey's disapproving expression.

'Betty,' Audrey said, in a serious, hushed tone, 'what on earth is going on? As a representative of Barton's bakery, this is no way to conduct yourself in the street! Christine, are you all right?'

Betty glared at Christine, who had started to whimper and was massaging her wrist as though Betty had been too rough with her. With her eyes open wide, she blinked innocently at Audrey, shaking her head.

'She attacked me, Mrs Barton,' said Christine. 'I only came in to say that I remembered where I'd seen Betty before. She's not from Portsmouth. As her employer, you should be aware that she's not who she says she is. She's on the run from Bristol and has secrets she's not willing to share with us.'

In that moment Betty despised Christine. What would she gain from blowing Betty's cover? Just when she was beginning to love her job, too.

'Is this true?' said Audrey, hands on her hips. Betty opened her mouth to answer but couldn't find any words. Feeling cornered and diminished by the disappointment in Audrey's questioning gaze, she quickly pulled off her bakery overall and cap, stuffed it into Audrey's arms and ran down Fisherman's Road towards the sea.

*

'I can't believe she attacked me. I feel ever so shaken up,' said Christine dramatically, batting her eyelids and straightening the collar of her dress. 'I only called in to say goodbye and look what happened!'

Audrey studied Christine's features and found her to be quite unconvincing. There was something about the girl's tone she didn't trust – but she'd seen what had happened herself. Despite being the size of a sparrow, Betty had thrown Christine up against the wall and was clearly threatening her, though she wouldn't really call it an attack. Always instinctively wanting to defend the underdog, Audrey was tempted to insist that Betty must have had a reason to behave so out of character, but she bit her tongue and shook her head.

'I don't know what's going on, but I'll find out,' she said, before taking Christine's hand and gently shaking it. 'It's been lovely to meet you, Christine. I wish you luck returning to Bristol. This war has torn apart some of our most beautiful cities but in time hopefully they will be rebuilt. I do hope you can get on with your life there now you've had some respite here.'

At the change of subject and mention of her home, a wave of emotion passed over Christine's face, and Audrey's heart went out to her. Wartime was hard on everyone. Bidding her farewell, Audrey's mind returned to Betty. After checking that Lily and Pat could watch the shop, she set off in the direction Betty had dashed off, walking as quickly as her pregnant bump would allow.

'She didn't get far,' she muttered to herself when she spotted Betty sitting in the long grasses on the clifftop, her chin leaning on her knees. Pausing for a second to admire a common blue and clouded yellow butterfly, Audrey felt heartened – they carried on fluttering about despite the ugly sea defences, pillboxes and rolls of barbed wire on the beach below. As she continued towards Betty, she was hit once again by a pain in her lower back so sharp that she had to pause, close her eyes for a moment and take a deep breath.

After a few moments the pain eased and she reached Betty, who turned to face her with tear-stained cheeks.

'Dry those tears,' said Audrey, lowering herself to the ground with difficulty and resting her palm on Betty's shoulders, 'and tell me what's troubling you.'

Chapter Eight

With Audrey waiting patiently for her to speak, Betty drew a shuddering breath and wiped her eyes with the backs of her hands. She barely knew Audrey, but there was something about the woman that could cut through a person and directly reach their heart, like a hot knife through butter. There was no point trying to tell her any more tales; she would only dig herself a deeper hole to fall into and have to claw herself out of. Plucking at the grass beneath her feet and throwing it down again, she struggled to find the right words. Sitting on the clifftop like this, among the wild sea-pink flowers and the yellow gorse, with picture postcard views stretching across the bay to Old Harry Rocks and the Purbeck Hills, she felt completely disorientated.

'I do believe that's a peregrine falcon,' said Audrey, pointing to the large bird of prey with a blue-grey back and a black head hovering in the sky. 'You don't see many these days. They used to be on the protected list, but they've been attacking pigeons carrying vital services messages, so the government have taken them off the list. They're being shot now, and their eggs taken out of nests and destroyed. Another sacrifice of war.'

'That's sad,' mumbled Betty. 'I hadn't thought that the war would affect birds too.'

Audrey nodded, and they sat together in silence for a few moments before she placed a hand on Betty's arm and patted it, reassuringly.

'Why don't you begin with telling me where you're really from, Betty?' she said. 'And, is Betty your real name?'

'Yes,' replied Betty with a sigh. 'I'm from Bristol. I've never even been to Portsmouth.'

Thoughts of her childhood and family in Bristol assailed Betty's mind. There was no denying that she'd had a rough start in life, raised in an orphanage after her mother died of consumption when she was three years old. The one and only memory she had of her mother was of bright patterned cloth, possibly a dress, or an eiderdown perhaps. Sometimes in her dreams she saw its joyful, vivid colours, and it was something to call her own, but how could she put all of that into words?

'I was born in Bristol,' was all she said. 'I grew up in an orphanage.'

She remembered how surprised she'd been when nobody at the orphanage read her a bedtime story. The place taught her strict discipline and how to scrub floors until they shone – the hours spent working trained her well for life in the tobacco factory, where she worked from the age of fourteen. She had nothing when she met Robert, and when he proposed after they'd courted for a few months, she didn't hesitate for a second. They'd moved in with his mother, into the house on Queen Street, and she finally had the family life she'd craved. She longed for kiddies to shower with love, to give them a better life than she herself had had so far, but what did she get instead? Robert's double-crossing and his shameful lie.

'So why did you say you were from Portsmouth?' asked Audrey, frowning.

'Because I've run away from Bristol,' she said. 'I've run away from my husband. His name's Robert and he's no good. He's… he's only gone and…'

Audrey put her arm round Betty's shoulders and Betty had to use all of her might to hold in the floods of tears that were threatening to spill. A few leaked onto her cheeks regardless.

'Oh Betty,' said Audrey. 'I've seen the way some husbands treat their wives, beating them black and blue. Cutting them off from their friends and family. I've had customers who have been married to rotten men and regretted their decision. Personally, I wouldn't stand for it. I'd run away like you and find a way to escape the violence—'

'It's not that,' interrupted Betty, suddenly feeling strangely protective of Robert again. 'He's never raised a finger to me. No, it's, well, it's… I must have been doing something very wrong, because he's got another woman, hasn't he? I say another woman but it's not like he's got a fancy woman, no, it's worse, he's, he's… he's got a wife and kids. He's married to two women, would you believe? Ha! Two wives in the same city and all.'

'Well I never,' Audrey gasped. 'What a swine! Not to mention criminal! He could go to prison for that. Bigamy, it's called. I read about a local case in the paper. How long have you known that, you poor dear girl?'

'A few weeks. I came here because I couldn't stand it any longer,' Betty said. 'I'd rather have gone anywhere than stay there feeling angry and upset and ashamed. Sometimes, when he came home and sat down in front of the fire to listen to the wireless, he'd ask me to massage his shoulders because they were stiff from working at the dockyard, and do you know what, Mrs Barton?'

Audrey shook her head sadly while Betty blinked away her tears.

'I did it!' she said, thumping the ground with her hand. 'I'd obediently rub his shoulders and watch him close his eyes in pleasure and all the time I didn't say a word about what I knew! I'm a coward, that's what I am. I should have hit him on the head with the fire poker!'

Chewing the inside of her cheek, she shook her head in anger at herself and batted away a fat bee that seemed determined to land on her dress.

'No,' said Audrey, sighing. 'You're not a coward. It's sometimes impossible when you know what you're about to say will blow your life apart – it's easier just to carry on carrying on. We've all done it in some way or another, love. Oh Betty, my heart goes out to you. Is this what the problem was with Christine? Does she know Robert?'

'Yes,' Betty said. 'Her husband is a friend of his. I thought about telling her the truth, then I worried that she'd tell everyone and Robert would go to jail. I hate him, but I don't want to see him behind bars. Anyway, when I wouldn't tell her the truth, she threatened to tell him where I am unless I paid her half my wage. I lost my temper.' She stared away, at the ground.

'I would have lost mine too,' said Audrey. 'How dare she try to blackmail you? I wouldn't have believed she had it in her, until today. Surprising how folk can be, isn't it? Ouch!'

Betty turned to look at Audrey, who was holding a hand against her bump and frowning, perhaps as if the baby had kicked her. She relaxed and smiled again. 'It's nothing,' she said. 'Ignore me.'

'If you want me to leave, I will,' said Betty, thinking that even though Audrey had been sympathetic about her plight, she would probably now distrust her for lying, but Audrey shook her head.

'Don't be ridiculous! I want you to get back to the shop and start working the rest of your shift,' she said. 'You've done enough running. Stay put in Bournemouth and we'll work out what to do together. Sounds like you could do with a friend, Betty.'

It was the first time anyone had used the word 'we' or 'together' in relation to her for a long time. Overwhelmed with gratitude and with a feeling of warmth in her heart, she quickly stood up, brushed off her dress and offered a hand to Audrey, helping her to her feet.

'Thank you,' said Betty. 'Thank you from the bottom of my heart.'

Despite Audrey's kindness, Betty still felt a sense of unease as, after helping Pat with the WVS book collection, she walked home alone. It had been a long day and now, because of the blackout, the journey back to her rented room in complete darkness felt intimidating. Holding her breath as she passed dark doorways and narrow alleyways, Betty almost jumped out of her skin when a black cat leapt off a garden wall into her path.

'Silly moggy!' she hissed at the cat, resting her hand on her heart, which was pounding in her chest. 'Frightened me half to death.'

Telling herself to get a hold of her nerves, she focussed on how the air in Bournemouth seemed to always smell of fish and chips frying, and how tonight, it was pierced with the bright chorus of trumpets and trombones of 'In The Mood', a Glen Miller song. An echo of excited laughter, both male and female, erupted as the song finished and Betty half-smiled, imagining an energetic dance party somewhere in the town, keeping up morale and helping people forget the war for a few hours. Feeling slightly envious of the girls in their flowing dance frocks and heeled shoes, who could leave their troubles at the door of the dance hall, she battled with the unshakeable fear she felt about Christine, who would have been back in Bristol hours ago. Would she have gone to the docks to find Robert? Was she that spiteful? Or was she all talk? Betty shuddered, hoping that Christine would keep her nose out of it and her trap shut.

Approaching her digs – which in blackout would be impossible to see if it wasn't for the stripe of white paint the owner had painted on the gate to help tenants find their way – she was suddenly startled by the outline of a man lurking in the doorway of the Hotel Metropole. Heart hammering and her teeth chattering with nerves, a horrible thought suddenly dawned on her…

'What if it's Robert?' she whispered to herself. 'Come to get his money back.'

Before she had time to turn on her heel and run away as fast as she could, the figure leapt out of the doorway into her path. Closing her eyes, she screamed, but stopped when the man rested a hand on her shoulder and spoke in a friendly Canadian accent.

'Hey, hey, Betty, it's Sam!' he said, laughing gently. 'I'm so sorry I scared you. I've been waiting for you for an hour. Are you okay?'

Hand on her chest, cheeks puffed out as she exhaled, she took a moment to recover before standing up straighter, glaring at Sam for frightening her.

'What were you doing, hiding in the shadows like that?' she cried. 'You terrified me! Thought it was someone out to get me, didn't I?'

Sam pulled a sad face and put his head on one side.

'I'm sorry. I was just waiting for you, that's all, because it's my birthday,' he said. 'There's a dance on and I wanted to ask if you'd come along. I'd love you to come with me.'

He gently grabbed her hand and tugged her a few steps along the pavement and for a split second she almost let herself go, before remembering.

'I can't,' she snapped, shaking off his hand, pushing past him, throwing open the front door, which was always unlocked, and running up to her bedroom. Wrestling with the key in the lock, muttering under her breath, she finally let herself in and slammed the door behind her. The room was dank, dark and unwelcoming. Feeling torn apart with guilt, she saw Sam's crushed expression in her mind's eye. Why had she been so rude to him, on his birthday too?

With tears stinging her eyes, she quickly walked to the window and opened it slightly, peering outside. 'Oh Sam,' she whispered, hoping he'd still be out there so she could call out an apology, or at least offer him a small wave, but he was gone. The street was empty. Dejected, she moved away from the window and sat on the edge of the creaky bed, feeling like the loneliest person in the world. She imagined Sam joining the noise, laughter and music at the party, dancing with another girl who was light and quick on her feet, with a pretty dress and a beguiling smile – she knew it would only be a matter of time before he forgot that she even existed. She let out a deep sigh and closed her eyes. She was getting what she wanted after all: to be invisible.

Chapter Nine

Elsie had it all planned. She'd waited until Sunday, when, after roasting the neighbourhood's Sunday dinners in the falling heat of the bakery ovens, William would have a few hours away from his duties at the bakehouse before scraping out the fat, cleaning and relighting the ovens for the week ahead. Wearing a frock she knew William liked, she had washed her hair with soap flakes and pinned it up and had applied leg make-up and a dash of red lipstick. While working her sixty-hour week on the buses Elsie didn't have the time to wear make-up, but this was a special occasion. Glancing at her reflection in the bottom of a copper pot hanging on the kitchen wall, she frowned. A lot rested on this day.

'Are you ready then?' she said to William when he came into the kitchen on his crutches, newly shaved and dressed in his Sunday best. Because of clothes rationing his Sunday best was now the suit he wore any day of the week – and to do all manner of odd jobs around the bakery too – but he still looked smart. It was the same for most men and they weren't even allowed turn-ups on their trousers now because it was a waste of fabric. He sat down for a moment and smiled at Elsie, who lifted her finger to her lips as she moved closer to the wireless to hear the end of the Radio Doctor's advice on salad veg. She joined in with the popular ditty:

When salvage is all that remains of the joint
And there isn't a tin and there isn't a point
Instead of creating a dance and a ballad
Just raid the allotment and dig up a salad!

With a grin, she held out her hands and stamped her foot as if to say: 'Ta da!'

'Ha! Very good.' William laughed, clapping. 'Yes, I'm ready. So, are we having salad in our picnic?'

Elsie smiled, nodded, turned off the wireless and picked up the wicker picnic basket, draped in a tea towel embroidered with blue flowers. Slung over her arm was her gas mask case, which she never failed to take with her, even though she'd noticed that some young people were getting lazy about remembering theirs.

'Just a salad sandwich,' she said, thinking of the carrot filling she'd mixed with mustard sauce and a dash of vinegar. 'But it'll do. Come on, we won't go far. I know you're busy later.'

'I have a whole list of things John has asked me to see to in the bake-house,' said William, 'but we deserve an hour or two together, don't we?'

With posters pasted up bearing slogans such as 'Three words to the WHOLE NATION: Go To It!' on every corner, it was easy to feel guilty about having a few hours off from your war work and duties, even on a Sunday, but this was important.

'Yes, we do,' she said, standing on tiptoe so she could kiss him lightly on the lips.

Though she was pretending to be carefree that morning, she felt daunted by the task ahead. William's horrific nightmares were not abating, and it was time for Elsie to get to the bottom of the problem. She'd made a promise to herself that she'd ask him outright – it was now or never.

*

'I'll leave the door open,' Audrey called to William and Elsie as they left the bakery backyard and made their way to the clifftop. She was on her hands and knees, scrubbing the back step, and would move on to swilling out the yard.

'Thanks, Sis,' said William. 'Oh, and don't think I haven't remembered it's your birthday this week!'

Audrey stopped scrubbing for a moment and leaned back on her haunches, tucking a stray strand of hair behind her ear.

'Is it?' said Elsie, her eyes wide. 'You haven't mentioned it, Audrey!'

'Oh, I don't want to be bothering with my birthday,' said Audrey. 'Too much to do. Our mother never used to bother much with my birthday and that's the way it's always been. We might have had a jam tart for tea, but nothing else.'

'Not a cake?' said Mary, who was crouching next to Audrey, helping to scrub the baking tins, setting them out in rows on the ground to let them dry in the sunshine. It was a mucky job – the little girl's face, arms and knees were covered with black smudges and she would need a dunk in the tin bath afterwards – but she was happy to be busy and helping. If truth be told, that had been Audrey's way of helping Mary endure all the grief she'd suffered since arriving at the bakery as an evacuee – she had learned to keep the girl engrossed in a job, whether it be helping make a rag rug, preparing the rabbit stew or helping to black the range.

'No, love, even though I make them most days,' said Audrey, with an amused smile. 'But I don't mind a jot.'

'That might be so,' said William, 'but you could at least have an hour off the hard work. You shouldn't be working so hard in your condition.'

'Oh, be gone with you,' said Audrey, then, when they were out of earshot, whispered 'Good luck, Elsie,' to herself. Audrey had told Elsie to talk to William about the death of his friend and she was worrying about how he would take it. Charlie had sometimes used to say she stuck her nose in where it wasn't wanted, but Audrey couldn't sit back and watch her brother and his new wife go on suffering. Life was too short, especially in these times. Returning to her scrubbing, but now thinking of Charlie, she physically longed to hear from him. It had been months since she'd written to break the news of her pregnancy, and she'd written twice again since, but there had been no reply.

She couldn't help thinking about the stomach-churning story she'd heard from one of her customers whose son, held in a Nazi prisoner-of-war camp, had been forced to eat bread made of sawdust. Audrey suspected that this was likely only one of the trials their soldiers were facing, but the thought of strong men starving near to death deeply affected her. Putting a meal on the table, however humble, was what she did, so to think that Charlie might not even have anything to eat… oh, it didn't bear thinking of.

Keep safe, Charlie, she thought, pausing in her scrubbing again for a moment as she was hit by a bolt of pain in her lower back that made her drop the scrubbing brush. It skittered across the yard. Audrey tried to sit back again but instead fell onto her side. She closed her eyes and drew her knees up to relieve the pain.

'Oh no!' said Mary, trying to throw her little arms round Audrey, her brown eyes full of concern. 'Shall I call Old Reg? Or fetch the smelling salts?'

Seeing the distress on Mary's face, Audrey gritted her teeth against the pain and forced herself to smile from her ungainly position on the floor.

'Don't worry anyone, Mary love, it's Sunday,' she breathed, trying to sit upright but failing. 'Help me up to sitting, will you? I'll be all right in a minute.'

'Wait,' said Mary, jumping up and dashing into the Anderson shelter, from where she extracted a pillow and a flour sack. She gently pushed the pillow under Audrey's head, then laid the sack over her body, before racing upstairs to the kitchen, leaving Audrey where she had fallen, gripped by terror as she waited, desperately, to feel her baby move. Hardly daring to breathe, she held her hand over her bump, praying and begging for it to poke her with an elbow, knee or ankle. After an agonising few moments, it did. Relief coursed through Audrey's veins.

'I've got you some tea,' said Mary, who had reappeared, walking towards her and bending down, with tea sloshing out of the cup and into the saucer that she'd so carefully carried downstairs. 'Don't worry, I didn't make fresh and waste the rations. There was some left in the pot. The "dregs" as Uncle John calls it.'

Audrey smiled, knowing that the teapot had been standing for hours. But now that the pain had subsided a little, she was able to sit up and lift the cup of cold, weak tea to her lips.

'Thank you, Mary, love, it's delicious,' she said, blinking in the sunlight. 'I think I'll be all right now. The pain has gone.'

'You're awfully pale,' said Mary, inspecting Audrey's face so closely their noses almost touched, resting her little cool hand on Audrey's forehead. Audrey smiled and chuckled. Her heart swelled at Mary's sweet ways, but she didn't want the girl to be worrying. Though her own head was awash with anxiety, she knew she couldn't let the thoughts in her head show on her face.

'I'm right as rain now,' she said. 'Don't worry.'

'Are you sure?' asked Mary.

'Yes, I'm absolutely fine,' Audrey said, taking hold of Mary's hand and squeezing it. At that moment, Lily came into the backyard singing, carrying Joy in her arms. On seeing Audrey under a flour sack with her back against the bakery wall and the tins scattered around her feet, her face fell and she stopped singing.

'What's happened?' she said, gently putting Joy down to toddle towards Mary, who held her arms outstretched. 'Do you need a doctor?'

Audrey felt her eyes fill with tears, but tutted and rapidly blinked them away. She never cried in front of anyone else and wouldn't start now.

'No, I don't! I can manage perfectly all right on my own. Besides, what would he say?' she said, wearily. 'The baby's still moving, so he or she is fine. I don't want to bother the doctor. I've only a matter of weeks left now, so I think it's probably just that when the baby moves into a certain position, he or she is pressing on something. The little monkey!'

She managed to raise a smile and held her hand out so Lily could help her up to standing. Back on her feet, the bakery yard seemed to spin around as if she was on a merry-go-round. She blinked several times, focussing on the crop of leeks that burst out of the soil on top of the Anderson shelter like the few strands of hair that stuck up on Uncle John's head. Eventually, the spinning slowed down and her vision was clear.

'You should stop working so hard,' said Lily. 'We've got Betty to help in the shop now and William and Uncle John in the bakehouse. I can do more shifts as well as my work at the library. Albert is out delivering but he could do more in the bakehouse if you needed him. Please promise me you'll see the doctor. If you don't promise me, I'll see him for you.'

Disliking being told what to do and not being able to stand the thought of working less at her beloved bakery, Charlie's family's business, Audrey felt a ripple of irritation pass through her.

'Stop fussing,' she said, 'and please do leave me alone to make my own decisions. Right now, I better sort out these tins, sweep out the shelter and bathe Mary before the day gets away from me.'

Lily looked a little hurt, but Audrey hated fuss more than anything and didn't want her pregnancy to be viewed as a weakness. Hands on her hips, she looked around the yard at the tins on the floor, the Anderson shelter door swinging on its hinges and Joy pulling the head off a daffodil growing in a pot. She sighed, making a mental list of things that needed doing, and reached for the broom. She began to sweep the floor of the shelter, all the while aware that Lily, Mary and Joy were watching her.

'Are you going to give me a hand then?' Audrey quipped with a smile. 'Or just stand there gawping?'

*

After they'd eaten their sandwiches, Elsie leaned back on her elbows and gazed out to sea. Under the cloudless sky, the sea looked blue and inviting and as the sun warmed her bare legs and feet, Elsie was reminded of courting William during the pre-war days. Picnics on the beach, swimming and a game of beach cricket – she could almost hear the echoes of their laughter.

'If you close your eyes and listen to the murmur of the sea and the cry of the gulls,' she said, squinting, 'you can almost imagine that there are paddlers, rubber floats and swimmers in the sea, and that Bournemouth was back to normal and there had never even been a war.'

Rubbing her toes together, she waited for William to respond, aware that she'd probably said the wrong thing. How could he ever imagine there had never been a war when his body and mind were so badly injured?

'If I close my eyes,' said William, quietly, 'all I can see are ghosts.'

'Oh, I'm sorry, William,' Elsie said, tenderly. She sat upright, tucked her feet under her bottom and faced him, her eyes flickering over his scarring.

'That was stupid of me. I didn't mean that,' she said. 'I know neither you nor any of us can ever forget the war. It's all around us, every day. It's on our minds when we wake up and when we go to sleep. It's become a part of us and it'll define our lives. It's turning us into different people.'

William sighed and turned his gaze away from Elsie. She fiddled with the tassel trim of the blanket, her heart hammering in her chest, knowing that she should ask him now, outright, to tell her about what happened in France. Staring at her wedding band, she wondered why she was so frightened to ask. What could he possibly say that would change how she felt about him? Heartened by that thought, she reached for his hand and wrapped her fingers round his.

'William,' she said softly. 'The nightmares you've been having, will you tell me about them? Audrey mentioned that something happened while you were away. I mean, something other than the bomb that hit your truck – about a man called David?'

'Audrey said what?' William snapped, glaring at her and shaking his hand free of hers. 'She'd no right to say anything! I talked to her in confidence.'

Inside, Elsie felt dejected and slightly impatient, but she swallowed her hurt and tried again. She wasn't going to give up on this now.

'Please,' she said, tucking her black hair behind her ears. 'I need to know what's on your mind. I might be able to help, or at the very least understand you better.'

William pushed himself up to standing with the aid of his crutches and shook his head. Whenever he did that, his shirt came untucked, which she knew he hated. It was all she could do to stop herself from helping him tuck it back in.

'I just want to help,' she said quietly, aware that her words weren't going down well. 'Let me help you, for goodness' sake. I'm your wife!'

'But how can you help?' he said, his expression dark. He angrily knocked over a cup with his crutch, spilling the lemonade onto the rug, and Elsie bit her lip to stop herself reacting. She picked up the cup and stared up at him, her eyes shining.

'You've got no idea about anything, Elsie,' he continued. 'You think you're helping with the war effort, punching tickets on that bus of yours, but you've never dodged death by running into fox-holes like a terrified animal, you've never watched men get blown up into bits all around you, your friends decimated before your very eyes! You've never collected up their body parts with shaking, blood-soaked hands, just so there was something to bury! You've never, you've never...'

Elsie's throat thickened and she swallowed hard, feeling the colour rise in her cheeks. Instructing herself to be strong enough to shoulder his blame and anger, despite it being misplaced, she stood to face him, a gentle breeze lifting her skirt to her knees.

'I've never what?' she said firmly. 'Tell me, William.'

With his good leg, he kicked at a stone on the floor.

'You've never made a dreadful decision and been responsible for your friend's death!' he roared, now throwing one of his crutches onto the floor and collapsing back down onto the picnic blanket, covering his face with his hands. 'You've never been a yellow-belly coward! It's worse than being a dead man! I would rather be a dead man!'

Crouching beside him as his body shuddered with angry sobs, Elsie rested her palm on his back and, lost for words, tried to communicate through the heat of her hand. When he looked up again, his eyes were bright red and haunted with images of violence. He wiped his nose on the back of his hand and glared at Elsie, but his eyes were unfocussed, as if he were looking at something else. Elsie was taken aback by how pitiful, how pathetic, he looked.

'I don't understand,' she said quietly.

'I made a terrible mistake,' he said, his voice flat. 'I came face-to-face with a young German soldier. I was inches from him. I didn't shoot him, I let him go. He looked so young. Moments later, he turned back and shot my friend, David, in the stomach and chest. I watched David die in agony. He was so young. His mother's only son. It was my fault that he died, Elsie. I'm a coward. You married a coward.'

'No,' she said, her voice breaking as tears spilled from her eyes. 'I married a good man. That… that was a moment, a split-second decision. You chose to be compassionate and it wasn't reciprocated.'

Elsie swiped at her tears, not wanting him to see how his story had affected her. Her head ached, and her thoughts were foggy. She tried to put herself in his shoes; she could completely understand his guilt. She would feel the same, she knew that. Was there any escape?

'I've been trying to put it behind me,' he said, staring at the horizon. 'I feel cruel, telling you all of this. I've been trying to be a man and not lay this dreadful story at your feet, but his image haunts me. The sound of David's cry as he lay dying rings in my head like the toll of a church bell. I keep telling myself to keep a stiff upper lip and get on with it, like the older generation who fought in the Great War do, but the truth is I feel wretched. I can't stop myself returning to that dark place, to try to make sense of it. Of course, I never can.'

'Perhaps it's braver to let yourself go to that dark place and experience those dark feelings,' said Elsie. 'You don't have to hold it all in. Let yourself grieve.'

William shook his head. Elsie knew her words were falling on deaf ears.

'It's his mother,' William said. 'She doesn't know that just before he died he was talking to me about his home and how he'd always be grateful to his mother for giving him a happy childhood. I keep thinking that I should visit her to tell her, but I expect it's a terrible idea. Perhaps she's better off for not knowing the truth. She would despise me, at the very least.'

Elsie thought about it for a few moments before reaching for his hand.

'I'll come with you if you decide to go,' she said. 'I think a mother would want to know the facts, no matter how painful for you and her.'

William's face paled. He stared down at the picnic blanket.

'What you said earlier, about the war changing us,' he said, 'you were right. I have changed. The war has near ripped out my heart and replaced it with stone.'

Elsie felt the weight of William's misery bearing down on her like lead as she folded up the picnic blanket and tucked it under her arm. Delving deep into her own reserves of strength, she found a reassuring smile for him.

'We'll find a way,' she said. 'We're in this together. You're not alone.'

William's nostrils flared. He was obviously stopping himself from getting emotional and, eventually, he managed a small smile, a dim light flickering in his eyes. He opened his mouth to speak but clearly couldn't find the words.

'Let's walk back to the bakery,' Elsie suggested, 'and make a plan.'

Chapter Ten

Pat's face was partly obscured by the precarious tower of twenty books she carried into the foyer of the Metropole Hotel. With her heart in her mouth, Betty followed her closely, arms outstretched and ready to catch any flying novels. Stepping into the hotel entrance, where pungent lilies in an enormous blue and white vase drooped in the heat, Betty tucked her hair behind her ears, discreetly pinched her cheeks and swept her eyes over the reception area and the drawing room, in case Sam was there.

'Make a space, Betty!' Pat commanded, as they approached a table where a small collection of books had already been deposited. Betty quickly cleared a space and began to lift down the donated books a few at a time from Pat's tower and display them on the table.

'Why are your hands shaking, lovey?' Pat asked. Betty just shrugged and rubbed them together.

'They're cold,' she mumbled.

'Cold?' shrieked Pat. 'It's warm as toast in here. Anyway, get on with it, we don't have all night.'

Betty let out a small exasperated sigh and continued with the job. As she did so, a small crowd of Canadian soldiers and airmen gathered, dressed in their perfectly pressed, smart blue uniforms, stopping to read the descriptions on the backs of the books or flick through a few pages. Though she tried not to, Betty blushed at the sight of the men and once more scanned the room for Sam, but he was still nowhere in sight.

Relief and disappointment coursed through her. After the incident the other evening, when she'd been so rude to Sam on his birthday, she thought it best that she avoided him altogether. When Pat had announced they were delivering books to the hotel after her shift at the bakery had ended, her stomach had turned in on itself, but she had convinced herself that he had most likely forgotten all about her and was probably out with a pretty young woman who he'd met at the dance. Or perhaps he'd already been posted on operational service. These men were only in Bournemouth for a short period of retraining and orienteering before joining a squadron. Chances were that she'd never see him again – ships passing in the night and all that.

'Betty,' said a familiar male voice, interrupting her thoughts. 'I'm beginning to suspect you're following me. We really should make this official and go on a date…'

Gaping at Sam, Betty dropped the books she was holding and blushed madly, hit, not for the first time, by how handsome he was, with his blond hair, dark brown eyes, cheekbones sharp as knives and strong jawline. He towered above the other soldiers. Betty smiled up at him, her cheeks firing red, as he picked up the books she'd dropped and pretended to read from one of them.

'Once upon a time a young girl named Betty met a handsome fellow named Sam,' he started, giving her a winning smile. 'Sam was the envy of all the boys in the Canadian Air Force because he was the finest pilot they'd ever known. One evening, this heroic pilot asked Betty out, but Betty wasn't interested. He wanted to show her what he could do on the dancefloor…'

Sam threw a few dance moves, nearly knocking over the vase of lilies, and Betty put her hands to her mouth to suppress a hoot of laughter, but before she could stop giggling, Pat waded over in her sturdy brogues.

'And who, may I ask, are you, young man?' Pat said, positioning herself in between Sam and Betty, with her right hand raised in order to shake Sam's hand. Placing the book back down on the table with an amused expression on his face, he took a bow, shook Pat's hand and grinned.

'I'm Sam, and I arrived in this wonderful town with the Royal Canadian Air Force three weeks back,' he said. 'Betty and I have become acquainted since she's staying in the hotel next door. I was hoping, ma'am, that before I'm sent on an operation, Betty might accompany me for an evening out. Am I right in thinking that you're her sister? It can get a little dreary with all these fellas, what with our lectures on flying and all. A man needs to have a little fun.'

Pat tutted, put her arms behind her back and rocked on the balls of her feet.

'Of course I'm not her sister! You should keep your eye on the job, young man,' she said. 'Have you seen what Jerry has done to this country? We need men like you to help, not get distracted by a pretty young face like Betty here.'

Betty blushed, hoping that Sam wouldn't take offence at Pat's comments. She hadn't known the woman long, but already knew that she couldn't help but wade in and stick her nose in, whether it was wanted or not.

'Oh, but a pretty face and good conversation are so good for morale, Mrs…?' Sam said.

'Barton,' said Pat. 'Mrs Patricia Barton.'

'Mrs Barton,' said Sam. 'My mind is always on the job. How can it not be? I've sailed thousands of miles from home, of my own free will, to put my military training to good use and help defeat Hitler, to win peace and freedom for us all. I don't mean any harm by letting off a little steam and taking a pretty girl to a dance. I'm a gentleman through and through. Betty knows that, don't you, Betty?'

Betty, lost for words, nodded and busied herself with arranging the books. Pat, seemingly humbled by his words, looked apologetic and mumbled, 'Of course,' before continuing with her task.

'Anyway, I'm making a nuisance of myself, so good day to you, ma'am,' he said. 'Good to see you, Betty.'

He began to walk away, and Betty tried not to stare at his physique beneath his jacket. He looked incredibly strong – like he could lift an aircraft, not just fly one.

'Come on, Betty,' said Pat, tutting. 'We need to get on with our next delivery. If you want my advice, keep away from flirts like Sam.'

Pat quick-marched out of the hotel first, and, managing to tear her gaze away from Sam's shoulders, Betty started to follow her. There was a tap on her arm and she turned to find Sam grinning at her. Eyeing Pat, he quickly handed her a piece of paper and winked.

'Betty!' called Pat from the van. 'Come on with you!'

Betty glanced at the piece of paper and saw that he'd written a message: To B, *6 p.m. at the clock tower, tomorrow. Jitterbug lesson. From S x*

Grinning, Betty stuffed the piece of paper into her pocket and ran towards Pat, who was waiting with an impatient look on her face, but not before she glanced back at Sam, gave just the slightest nod of her head and mouthed, *okay.*

*

Mary waited until Audrey was with Uncle John in the bakehouse, discussing tomorrow's bread orders, before she crept into the kitchen in stockinged feet from which one big toe had escaped. Tucking her silky bobbed hair behind her ears and with a mix of excitement and trepidation in her heart, she quietly opened the cupboards, searching for ingredients. Blinking into the dark cupboards that Audrey kept spotlessly clean and astonishingly organised, Mary breathed in the heady fragrances of baking: ginger powder, cinnamon and nutmeg, currants and treacle. Though she longed to delve her little fingers into the neatly wrapped packets of dried fruit and squirrel away fistfuls of the sweet treats, she knew they were reserves to be kept for the bakery's Christmas orders. Instead, she reached for the dried milk powder and pulled it out of the cupboard.

'Margarine, sugar, dried milk powder,' she muttered, carefully lining up the packets on the kitchen table. Realising she needed a bowl and spoon, she quietly moved across the kitchen, pausing when she heard the sounds of the neighbourhood's children playing out on the street. Throwing open the window, she stuck her head out to see what games they were playing and to check that those American soldiers weren't handing out sweets. Traffic light lollies were her favourite. Goodness knows where they found them but find them they did.

'Oi, Scary Mary!' shouted a voice from the street. Squinting in the sunset and hearing the seagulls overhead – a nice change from those noisy aircraft that seemed to drop in and out of the clouds like yo-yos – she scanned the faces until she recognised Billy, a bully boy from her class at school who smelled like soused herring and had once told her he weed on the raspberry bushes just after she'd picked and eaten some of the berries. Dressed in grey flannel shorts that were way too small on him, he called her 'Scary Mary' because once, when a siren had gone off while they were at school, Mary had been too scared to come out from under her desk. She hadn't been able to find the words to tell him what it was like to watch her brother die when a bomb had hit their home.

When he saw her, he stuck out his tongue, so she stuck out hers in return and slammed the window shut. Deciding she wasn't missing out on anything if he was there, she climbed onto a chair and poured the ingredients into a bowl. Creaming them together, she frowned – how was she going to make this cake look like a banana?

What can I use to make this yellow? she mused, returning to the cupboard and scanning the tins and packets, finally settling on a bright yellow tin of Colman's dried English mustard powder. That would do it! Though she wasn't sure how mustard powder would taste in icing, she decided to give it a go. Surely Audrey would be delighted with the banana cake even if it didn't actually taste like bananas. As she mixed in the mustard powder, the icing started to resemble a yellow sludge, but after spreading it onto the bread and shaping it into a banana shape, Mary was satisfied. She giggled, but was distracted by a stone being thrown up at the window.

'Billy, will you go away?' she muttered, licking her fingers and cringing at the flavour.

When another stone, bigger this time, hit the glass, Mary worried that he'd put a hole right through it, so she opened up the sash window and peered outside. The children had mostly gone and in Billy's place was a man three times his height, with broad shoulders and hands as big as saucepans.

'Sorry, miss,' he said. 'I saw someone was in there but couldn't get an answer at the door. I'm looking for Betty. Does she work here?'

Mary instinctively sensed danger but she was hopeless at acting and the man got the answer he wanted from her silence.

'I thought so,' he said. 'Do you know where she's staying? There's a shilling in it for you. Don't be frightened of me. I'm Betty's brother.'

Mary mulled over the man's words and stared at the coin in his palm. With that shilling she could buy Audrey a birthday present to show her how much she cared – and if he was Betty's brother, why wouldn't she want to see him?

'If you give me the shilling,' Mary said. 'I'll tell you.'

The man laughed.

'You're a smart one,' he said, tapping his skull. 'Now, where is she?'

'She's staying next door to the Metropole Hotel in town,' said Mary. 'You can catch the bus straight there. It's opposite the clock tower.'

'Good girl,' he said. 'Now keep this a secret, will you? I want to surprise her.' The man tossed the coin up into her hand and walked off down the road without waiting for an answer. Mary trembled, wondering now whether she'd made a mistake. Following him down the road with her eyes, she eventually tore herself away from the spot at the window and moved back to her cake, slipping the coin into her sock. The evening was warm, and the mock icing was already dripping unattractively down the sides of the bread. Hearing Audrey's footsteps on the wooden staircase, she quickly put a dish over the banana cake.

'Mary, were you talking to someone?' Audrey said, popping her head round the door. 'I thought I heard your voice.'

Mary thought about telling Audrey about the man for a second before shaking her head. She couldn't tell her the truth because then she wouldn't be able to keep the shilling and buy her a gift. No, she'd do as the man said and keep it a secret.

*

That night Betty got ready for bed with a knot of excitement and fear in her belly. Sitting at the tiny table at the end of her bed, which served as desk and dressing table, she studied the note that Sam had given her. Even his handwriting, which was like lace, was a little bit thrilling. Maybe it was wrong to have butterflies in her stomach, she thought, glancing at her pink cheeks in the small mirror hanging on the wall in the room, but she couldn't deny they were there. And why shouldn't she be thinking of enjoying herself for a change? With the war on – and after the shock of Robert's deception – she needed to let her hair down now more than ever before.

Tucking the note into the pages of the book Pat had given her, then spreading the colourful crochet blanket out on her bed, she thought of a speech that Winston Churchill had made on the wireless earlier in the week. Some of his words had stuck in her head: '… *we may stride forward into the unknown, with growing confidence*' he'd said. Of course, Churchill was talking about military operations, for which he had said '*there was only one end*', but somehow his words seemed to apply to her personal life too.

Before climbing into bed, Betty glanced out of the window criss-crossed with Splinternet tape and peered up and down the street, hoping there would be no air raid siren tonight. Just as she was about to turn away, a sudden movement in the bushes opposite caught her eye, making her suck in her breath and the hairs on her arms stand on end. She stared out into the darkness, thinking she could see something – or someone – staring back at her. Squinting, she rubbed her forehead and tutted.

'Robert?' she whispered, before shaking her head and rolling her eyes at herself, thinking that she was becoming paranoid. There was nothing and nobody there, just a seagull standing proudly on the clock tower.

Letting down the blind and sliding into bed, Betty wondered if she would ever be free from her fears or whether she'd always be looking over her shoulder, expecting Robert to have found her, wanting his money back. Shrugging off her anxiety, she pulled the blanket over her head and thought again about the note Sam had written. She would meet him tomorrow at 6 p.m. Whatever their meeting turned out to be, she was willing to give it a chance. If only for a few hours on one evening of her life, she would put the past behind her and live in the moment – striding forward into the unknown, with growing confidence.

Chapter Eleven

'There he is, the angel of death,' said Audrey to herself, standing outside the bakery in the sunshine, watching the young telegram messenger boy pedalling quickly over the potholes up Fisherman's Road on his red bicycle, the badge on his arm glinting in the early morning sunshine. Poor lad was only fourteen years old, if that, and his arrival at the front door was dreaded by everyone, in case he was delivering bad news from the War Office. As soon as they'd seen him coming people couldn't help staring at where the boy was headed, sometimes shouting out 'Telegram boy!' to warn their neighbours he was on his way, with their heads poking out of their windows, or waiting cross-armed at the garden gate as if standing guard. Sometimes the messenger boy would defy the nosy neighbours by going round the backs of the houses, down alleyways and through backyards – but either way, it didn't take long for news to get around. If you didn't hear the piercing scream of shock and grief from a woman given bad news about her husband or son, the news would still spread like wildfire in a blaze of whispers over the garden fence.

'Poor lad,' she whispered to herself. 'He carries a lot of responsibility on those young shoulders.'

Mind you, she thought, boys not much older were facing death in the battlefields, seeing goodness knows what. Every youngster was having to grow up so quickly these days.

'Mrs Barton?' said Freda, the postwoman, suddenly next to her, making Audrey jump out of her skin. 'Post.'

'Oh good heavens,' Audrey gasped when she realised she was holding out a letter. 'Thank you.'

Ripping open the envelope, her legs almost gave way as she recognised the handwriting and digested the words scribbled on one sheet of paper. It was from her dearest Charlie.

Audrey,

You know I'm not one for writing long letters, but I got your three letters all at once and I nearly fell off my chair when I read about the baby. After all these years... I can see the shop sign now: Barton & Son or Daughter. Look after yourself, dear girl. Let John do the lifting in the bakery. You're always in my thoughts and thinking of our life together at the bakery keeps me going. I am keeping all right here, so you mustn't worry about me.

Charlie x

Tears rushed into her eyes and she quickly blinked them away as a bolt of relief passed through her body. She clutched her throat. She felt like yelping in joy. It was the morning of her birthday and there couldn't have been a greater gift than Charlie's letter. Though, out of the corner of her eye, she could see the messenger boy knocking on the door of the poor cobbler and his wife at the other end of Fisherman's Road, and her heart broke for them, she couldn't deny her own sense of relief. Charlie was alive. Charlie knew about the baby. At long last he had written.

His letter, however, made her feel his absence like a wallop on the head, and she longed to hear his voice and throw her arms round him. Suddenly light-headed with emotion, she held onto the frame of the bakery doorway to recover her balance, then, staggering a little, walked back inside the shop. She clutched the letter in her hand, shaking her head in disbelief. After all these months of waiting, she'd finally heard from him. Betty stopped sweeping up crumbs and, leaning her hands on the broom handle, stared at Audrey in concern.

'Are you all right, Mrs Barton?' she said. 'Do you need to sit down? Have you had bad news?'

Audrey blinked. Music played quietly on the wireless and she felt as if time had stopped. All she could see and hear were Charlie's handwritten words. They were as clear in her mind as if he'd spoken them into her ear.

'No, thank you, Betty,' said Audrey quietly. 'I am perfectly well. In fact, I couldn't be better. Charlie has written to me and for now at least, I know he is safe.'

Returning to her position behind the shop counter, Audrey pulled the ledger book from the drawer of the wooden till and tucked the letter inside for safekeeping.

'That's wonderful news, Mrs Barton,' said Betty. 'I'm pleased for you. You must miss him very much.'

Audrey unconsciously patted her pregnant bump and smiled.

'I do,' she said, and saw sadness pass like a shadow over Betty's face. 'Oh Betty, I'm sorry. I know you have your own heartache to endure.'

'Actually,' said Betty, propping the broom up against the wall. 'A Canadian airman, called Sam, has invited me out tonight.'

Audrey's attention had been momentarily drawn by two women who were admiring the window display and pointing at the plaster of Paris wedding cake cover. Folk still thought they were real.

'Has he now?' said Audrey. 'And is this Canadian a handsome chap?'

'He is,' said Betty. 'I like him, but, as you know, I'm still married to Robert. Do you think it's okay if I…? Or does that make me as bad as him?'

The two women entered the shop, chatting to one another about the trials of shopping in wartime, and Audrey winked at Betty. 'I think it's okay,' she said, 'but I'd be honest right from the start. Hello, ladies,' she went on quickly, 'what can I get for you today?'

'Have you heard?' one said. 'We were just in the shop when the messenger boy came. The cobbler's boy is injured, but he's going to be okay. They had a telegram, see. I've never seen people so glad.'

Audrey closed her eyes in relief before realising the irony of the whole thing. The cobbler and his wife were glad that their son was injured rather than killed. That's how war made you: simply grateful to be alive.

Preparing the customer's order, she noticed the wide grin on Betty's face, and thought there must be something in the air today. Despite the horrors of war, there was a feeling of hope blowing around them, and even if it only lasted a day, or just a few hours, it was a reprieve for which Audrey was deeply grateful.

During the afternoon, the good weather broke. The sky over Southbourne turned pavement-grey, and unrelenting rain beat down against the bakery shop window, turning passers-by on the street into eerie dark blurs. The sea merged with the sky – but inside the bakery, the sun was still out and Betty hummed happily along to *Music While You Work* on the wireless. Though deep inside she feared that she might be playing with fire by going out with Sam, she couldn't wait for the evening. She hadn't felt this excited in a long while. After the terrible bombing in Bristol, the exploding skies and the crushed homes and dreams, she desperately wanted to feel like a normal young woman living a normal life. And, if Robert was enjoying himself with someone else, why shouldn't she? Their marriage vows meant nothing to him, so why should she remain tied to a man who didn't love her?

'This is a new start,' she told herself. 'I won't be held prisoner by Robert's lies.'

When Audrey let her go from work early, she burst out of the bakery and ran, with a newspaper over her head and splashing through puddles, towards the bus stop, where she planned to catch the bus back to her digs and change into a different dress. While waiting for the bus to arrive, she wiped the rain from her face and squeezed the water from her hair. She was dreaming of conversations she would have with Sam, wondering how best to explain her situation, when she felt a firm hand grip her arm. Her heart hammering in her chest, she cricked her neck and turned to face Robert. Unshaven, his hair unclipped and with dark bags under his eyes and his collar turned up, he looked like an unkempt villain who had been out on the ale.

'Betty,' he said, in a tone of voice that made her blood run cold. 'I've found you.'

'Get your hand off me,' she said, pulling at his fingers. 'You're hurting me.'

'You ain't seen nothing yet,' he said. 'You're my wife! You can't just up and leave me. Come with me. There's something I need to tell you.'

He yanked her arm again and pulled her away from the bus stop, frogmarching her down the road. Betty sighed bitterly, watching the bus and her evening with Sam disappear into thin air. How could she have ever imagined, even for a second, that she could enjoy an evening out with a dashing young Canadian? She was a married woman. She had run away from home. She had stolen money. Her newfound freedom was never going to last.

'Robert, I know all about you and Dor—' she started, but Robert was quick to interrupt and silence her with his words.

'You don't know nothing,' he said, gruffly. 'Just hear me out.'

*

Mary thought she would burst if she had to wait much longer. Bagging and selling the stales for a penny had taken for ever and now, watching Audrey turn the shop sign to closed and sweep up the crumbs from the floor, she impatiently shifted from one foot to another.

'Why are you acting so suspiciously, young lady?' Audrey asked her after they'd closed up the shop for the day. 'And where is everyone? I need to serve up dinner. We're having fish salad tonight, with a slice of yesterday's bread before it goes dry. That's my one complaint about the National Loaf, Mary, it's dry too soon. If there's any fish salad left, it'll do for fish and cabbage spread for Elsie's sandwiches tomorrow— oh, I believe it's Elsie's night off tonight, isn't it? I hope so. That girl works more hours a week than anyone else I know. She draws a good wage of course, but she deserves a break.'

Mary nodded obediently while Audrey chattered happily on, all the while clutching her small gift of a quart of pear drops bought from Old Reg, and a home-made card, behind her back. Lily had arranged for Elsie, William, Pat and Uncle John to be in the kitchen to surprise Audrey with a birthday tea, and it was Mary's job to keep her downstairs in the shop until they were ready at six o'clock on the dot. Burning a hole into the wall clock with her gaze, she couldn't hold her excitement in any longer. The second the big hand hit twelve, she jumped up and down on the spot.

'Happy birthday, Audrey!' she said, handing her the sweets and the card and throwing her arms round Audrey's expansive middle. 'Shall we go upstairs into the kitchen, so you can read my card with a cup of tea?'

'Oh Mary,' said Audrey, laughing and kissing the top of her head. 'Thank you. Aren't you thoughtful! But where did you get the money for these sweets?'

Mary felt herself blush, but she shrugged, gently pushing Audrey towards the stairwell and the kitchen.

'Come on,' she said. 'You must want some tea.'

'Okay,' said Audrey, laughing gently. 'But where is everyone?'

Mary's heart pounded in her chest as Audrey approached the kitchen door, more slowly than usual thanks to the baby growing in her belly. She so wanted to have got the surprise celebration right and could hardly wait to unveil her banana cake.

Hearing a muffled giggle followed by 'Shhh' as they approached the kitchen, Audrey turned round to look at Mary with an inquisitive grin on her face. Mary shrugged as if she didn't know anything and nervously watched Audrey place her hand on the doorknob and carefully open the door. When a rousing rendition of 'Happy Birthday' burst forth as Audrey walked into the room, she threw back her head and laughed out loud. William, accompanying on the mouth harp, finished the song with an impressive trill and everyone clapped and cheered.

'Oh Mary,' Audrey said, placing her hands on Mary's shoulders while she looked at the kitchen table where Elsie and Lily had been busy setting out a birthday tea. The tablecloth had been laid out on the kitchen table and the best glasses were turned upside down, waiting to be used. In the middle stood a plate of fish paste and cabbage sandwiches, and a jug of lemonade made with saccharine tablets was covered with a crocheted jug cover. Uncle John, with his white shirt sleeves rolled up, held out a chair for Audrey to sit down on and William tucked his mouth harp into his pocket. Dressed in a striped blouse, with her copper curls piled on her head, Lily handed Audrey a card and a small gift. And Pat, who had attached a brooch to her jacket and wore a pretty scarf round her neck, proudly handed her a knitted tea cosy.

'I made it for you,' said Pat. 'I hope you like it. I haven't wrapped it. Well, it would be wrong, what with the waste paper drive on.'

'I love it,' said Audrey. 'It's beautiful.'

'A man in my class made my gift,' Lily said, making everyone laugh, as Audrey unwrapped a small wood carving of a seagull.

'It's beautiful,' Audrey said, turning the seagull over in her hands. 'Thank you. Gracious, I'm bowled over by this!'

Mary beamed at Audrey, suddenly remembering the cake she'd made.

'There's something else too,' she said. 'Close your eyes and hold out your hands.'

Audrey closed her eyes as Mary placed a plate in her hands.

'Ooh, you're going to love this!' said Lily.

'You better share it with us,' said John. 'Don't be keeping it all for yourself!'

'Can I open my eyes now?' asked Audrey, cracking open one eye and staring in surprise at the plate, where there was a yellow blob of melted mock icing smeared over a length of bread, with a candle stuck in the middle. Registering Mary's expectant expression, full of hopeful anticipation, and feeling her heart might burst with gladness, Audrey broke out into joyful laughter.

'It's a banana cake,' said Mary, blushing. 'It's meant to look like a banana, but there's no banana in it!'

Audrey carefully placed the plate down on the table, smiled at Uncle John, who winked at her, and hugged Mary to her belly. She kissed her on the top of her head.

'Oh Mary, this looks quite delicious,' she said. 'How many years has it been since any of us has had a banana? Let me try a little piece.'

There was a moment of quiet as they all watched Audrey slice off a tiny piece and eat it. Audrey tried her hardest not to cringe, but the mustard powder was burning the roof of her mouth, and her cheeks were flushing boiling red.

'Gosh! Do I have steam coming out of my ears?' she spluttered. 'That's a very… unusual flavour, Mary. Is it mustard powder? Lots of mustard powder?'

Mary nodded. She covered her mouth with her hand but couldn't help bursting out into laughter. She was soon joined by everyone in the room, including Audrey, whose sides ached with laughing. For a brief wonderful moment, they were all laughing so hard it felt like they would never stop.

'Oh dear, oh dear,' said Audrey, wiping her eyes. 'Maybe I should make that one of our new wartime cakes! Certainly warm people up in the winter months!'

Still laughing, Audrey broke out into a cough, but then it stopped abruptly and she doubled over in pain, gripping the edge of the table to support herself. Pat, William, Lily, John and Elsie all immediately jumped up from their seats and moved towards her. A hush descended over the group.

'Are you unwell, Audrey?' Pat said, taking her arm. 'Is it the baby?'

Audrey felt the concern of everyone in the room like a warm, soft blanket, but she didn't want to ruin the occasion by worrying them.

'Goodness,' she gasped, forcing herself to smile. 'If there wasn't still a month to go, I'd think the baby was coming. He or she must be eager to get out!'

'Let me call the doctor out,' said Lily. 'I think you should tell him what's been going on. I'll run and get him. He won't mind.'

'Oh, please don't bother him,' said Audrey. 'He's such a busy man at the moment.'

'I will phone him and ask him to visit,' said Lily. 'You need to be honest about the pains you've been having. What if the baby's in trouble? Here, sit down.'

Suddenly feeling very unsure of herself, Audrey felt the fight drain out of her. She sat down heavily in the chair. Yes, maybe she did need to see the doctor. It was just that she could not bear to hear what he had to say. What if he gave her bad news?

'What pains? What's been going on?' said Pat, indignant. 'John, do you know about this?'

John, who had stuffed a sandwich into his mouth, didn't even finish chewing before he leapt to his own defence.

'What am I getting the blame for now?' he said. 'Course I didn't know! I would've been the first to tell her to get some help.'

'Well, you're here every day,' said Pat. 'Why didn't you notice that she's been having pains? I certainly would have done.'

'Oh well, you're bleeding perfect, Pat!' said John.

Audrey held her hands up to quieten everyone down.

'Nobody's to blame but me,' she said, fiddling with the edges of the tablecloth. 'It's true that I've had a few aches but they're not bad. The baby is moving – a lot – so surely that's all that matters?'

'What about you, though?' said Pat. 'You're just as important as the baby.'

'Listen, everyone, don't worry,' said Audrey. 'Let's enjoy these sandwiches before another siren goes off and we're stuck in the shelter.'

Audrey tried not to notice them all glancing anxiously at one another. Feeling Mary's hand slip into her own, she squeezed it gently to reassure her, though in truth, she felt suddenly vulnerable. All along she had been thinking about the baby and had been reassured that it was kicking and spinning around, but what about herself? Perhaps it would be wise to see the doctor, after all.

Later, Doctor Morris arrived in his smart, dark suit and, with Mary and Lily crowded into Audrey's bedroom, inspected Audrey's bump. Listening with his stethoscope for what felt like an inordinate amount of time, he felt all around her belly and asked her various questions, his thick black eyebrows knotted.

'I think you're suffering with heartburn, but it's also quite tight for space in there,' he said. 'That's why you're having pains. One of your nerves is getting in the way of the babies.'

'Baby,' Audrey quickly corrected him.

He raised an eyebrow and smiled a knowing smile, which confused Audrey.

'You said babies,' she said. 'It's baby. I'm having a baby.'

Chuckling a little, the doctor began packing away his equipment into his black doctor's bag and then sat on the edge of the bed, leaning across to pat Audrey on the hand.

'Mrs Barton,' he said. 'Do you know you're having twins?'

Audrey, now leaning with her back against the headboard, sat more upright as she tried to digest the doctor's words. Lily and Mary gasped.

'You mean…' stuttered Audrey. Her hand flew to her throat. 'Two babies?'

Her eyes scanned the room, briefly meeting Lily and Mary's before settling on the photograph of Charlie.

'Well, blow me,' she said. 'I don't know what to say or think! Two?'

'Twins.' Lily laughed. 'That's amazing!'

'Yes.' The doctor laughed as well. 'You're going to be a mother of two.'

'Three,' said Audrey, quick as a flash. 'I'm going to be a mother of three. Mary here is my eldest daughter.'

'Then you're going to have two siblings, young lady,' said the doctor to Mary, whose eyes had grown wide in her face. 'I'll arrange for an experienced midwife to come and visit you. Twin births are more dangerous, so we'll need to take good care of you.'

'Well I never,' Audrey said, stunned. She whispered into the room: 'How on earth will I manage?'

Lifting herself up to sitting, she tried to digest the news. Two babies. Charlie overseas. A war on and a bakery to run.

'Mrs Barton, if anyone can manage,' the doctor said with a smile, offering her a Nuttall's Mintoe to relieve the heartburn, 'I believe it's you.'

Chapter Twelve

Earlier that evening, Betty had had her own shocking news to digest. Standing in a puddle but not noticing the water soaking through the hole in the sole of her boot, with the wind and rain whipping against her face, making her skinny pale legs tremble, her jaw fell open as Robert told her his news.

'Doris is dead,' he said, speaking the words clearly causing him great pain. 'Bleedin' Jerry killed her when she was visiting her grandmother in Bath. Folk say the Luftwaffe were heading to Bristol again, but they emptied everything they had on Bath, late at night, when she had her head down for the night. She wasn't killed then, but at 4.30 a.m. when they came back. Course the fires were still blazing from the earlier raid and Doris was out trying to help the old folk get to safety. Firefighters did their best, but whole streets were alight, and so they hit it again, just to make sure. It was then that she was killed. Apparently, the pilots came so low folk said you could see their faces as they released the bombs.'

Betty had to sit down on a garden wall. She'd read in the papers about the latest attacks by the Luftwaffe, who had eased off very slightly from London and were pounding the historic towns of Bath, Norwich and York instead, apparently in retaliation for the RAF's hit on Rostow and Lubeck. Robert was a tough man. He worked long hours in the dockyards in all weathers until his hands were raw, and during the Bristol Blitz, he'd carried neighbours out of burning buildings over his shoulder without a moment's hesitation, giving them the clothes off his back if they needed them; but now, he was fighting back tears as he spoke. Betty was speechless. For so many weeks she'd felt furious with Robert for his double life and rogue ways, as he lied and cheated his way through their marriage. She'd hated him and Doris for having children that she'd so longed for and despised herself for not confronting them. But how could she feel hatred now? Seeing Robert like this broke her heart. Instinctively she wanted to comfort him – after all, he was her husband.

'Robert, I don't know what to say…' she started, reaching out for his hand and gently lacing her fingers through his. He squeezed her hand in his.

'Can I buy you a cup of tea out of the rain?' he said softly. 'You're soaked through. There's a café down here and I know I owe you an explanation.'

In the café, shivering in her damp summer dress, with the rain streaking the windows and a steaming cup of tea that she couldn't stomach in front of her, Betty's mind raced with questions. The wireless played in the background and the smell of toasted teacakes wafted through the room.

'About what's happened, Betty,' Robert said slowly, finally meeting her gaze. 'I know how this sounds, but it's been a tough few years.'

Betty shook her head and couldn't help rolling her eyes. Yes, the man was going through it, and she was sympathetic to that, but he'd been carrying on with another woman for years. She felt a tide of resentment rising in her.

'Perhaps you should have tried being honest,' she said quietly, tracing a flower pattern on the tablecloth with her fingertip.

'Thing is, I didn't know what to do,' he said, leaning back in his chair and looking out of the window. 'I was going with Doris before I met you and when we were married, she came to me and said she was expecting my child. Her dad threatened to wring my neck and kill me with his own bare hands if I didn't do the right thing by her, so I thought: nobody will find out, I'll marry her as well and help look after the wee one, while not letting you down. Trouble was that Doris fell with more babies and it got out of hand. I juggled two families. Course none of this was fair on you, I know that. You have every right to hate me. I've done wrong, I know that. But now Doris is dead, I want you to come home, so we can get back to normal.'

Betty almost laughed at Robert's naivety. Did he really expect she'd go running back to Bristol after the years of deception? Besides, she suddenly realised, he had three children. Unless…

'Oh Robert, were the children injured in the bomb?' she asked, her eyes open wide.

'No,' he said, shaking his head. 'Doris had left them with her sister in Bristol.'

Relieved, Betty exhaled, before asking: 'What will happen to them now? Will her sister take them in?'

Robert sighed and shrugged before scratching his head and loosening his shirt collar.

'I haven't worked that one out yet,' he mumbled. 'Will you come home, Betty love? That's what I came here to find out.'

Betty glanced at the clock on the café wall, where there was a poster declaring that 'Cadbury is Quality' next to a mirror, in which she caught her reflection. With wet hair stuck to her forehead and pink cheeks, she hardly recognised herself – or the glimpse of Robert she could also see; he looked suddenly much older than his years. The time was twenty-five minutes past five. She was due to meet Sam on the hour – and she didn't want to let him down.

'I need some thinking time,' she said, pushing back her chair with a screech. Robert stayed where he was, rooted to his chair, apparently defeated and drained by everything that was happening. He was in a sorry state and in spite of every mistake he'd made along the way, Betty's heart went out to him. She patted him on the shoulder and opened the door to leave.

'Don't keep me hanging on,' he muttered as she left the café without another word, the door swinging shut behind her with a thud.

Willing the bus driver to travel faster and spend less time talking to every Tom, Dick or Harry that embarked, Betty checked the time with the passenger sitting next to her every few moments.

'It's still five minutes to six,' the elderly man said, with a gentle laugh. 'Are you meeting a young man, by any chance?'

Betty blushed flaming red.

'Oh no, I…' she started, but when he raised his eyebrows, she smiled. 'Yes.'

'Don't you worry,' he said, patting her hand as she gripped onto the handrail. 'If he's got any sense, he'll wait all night for you.'

'He's Canadian,' she blurted out. 'I'm not sure how long he'll be in Bournemouth, so I don't want to be late.'

Betty frowned at her own words, wondering what on earth she was talking about.

'Ah, I see,' said the old man, with amusement in his voice. 'The Canadians have been here a while already and I should think they're browned off at being here so long without seeing any action. They've too much time on their hands for leisure activities.'

He winked at her and she blushed scarlet.

'This is me,' she said, jumping up from her seat. 'Good night, sir.'

He raised his hand and gave her a small wave.

'Youth comes but once in a lifetime,' he said. 'Enjoy yourself.'

Running to the clock tower, where she could see Sam getting drenched in the downpour, thoughts of Robert and of everything he'd just told her tumbled through Betty's head. Unable to make sense of how she was feeling, she slowed down to a walking pace and took a deep breath. *Wait a moment,* she said to herself, pausing to tie her shoelace, *what am I doing here? Why am I meeting Sam, when Robert, my husband, has just asked me to return to Bristol? Do I still love Robert? Or has he destroyed any love I had for him with his duplicity? Do I owe it to him to give the marriage another chance?* And what about Sam, this new man she felt compelled to meet. How did she know he was trustworthy? Feeling utterly confused, she wondered if she should just return to her room, pull down the blackout blind and sleep, but Sam had already spotted her and was calling out her name.

'The heavens have opened!' he said, pacing towards her. 'I was going to suggest a walk, but we might just as well go for a swim.'

Her doubts vanished. She grinned at Sam and took in all the details about him. So smartly turned out, even in the rain – he'd clearly polished his boots and buttons, had scrubbed and shaved and slicked back his hair. His teeth were pearly white and a dimple appeared in his left cheek when he smiled, but it was his eyes she was really taken with. They seemed to hold her, like warm hands, when he fixed her with his gaze.

'Let's go to a dance,' he said, 'and get out of this rain. I want to teach you how to jitterbug. Unless you're hungry? We could eat first if you're hungry?'

Betty shook her head. In her mind a distant voice was whispering at her to tell Sam she couldn't go to a dance, that she'd just had awful news that someone close to her family was dead and that she needed time to think about her life. But the words didn't come.

'Yes, but I…' she said hesitantly. 'It's difficult, I'm in an awkward situation…'

She rubbed her forehead and chewed the inside of her cheek, but he grabbed her hand and pulled her in the direction of the town centre.

'Let's forget all our troubles tonight,' he said, seeming to read her mind. 'Let's be two young people going to a dance. Nothing more, nothing less. The war, Hitler, whatever – they can all go to hell for a few hours. I know I could do with having some fun. Agreed?'

Betty felt a smile stretch across her face.

'Agreed,' she said. 'I'd like that very much.'

She slotted her arm through his, pushed away the image of Robert that kept popping into her mind and focussed on Sam, this brave young man, so far from his home, so far from everything and everyone he knew. Just like her, he was reaching out for a friend in all the chaos and strangeness that was the spring of 1942.

'You're pretty good!' Sam laughed. 'You've done this before!'

'No, I really haven't!' Betty replied breathlessly as she grabbed the bottom of her skirt and swished it to the music, an energetic rendition of 'Bugle Boy', played by a local band. She had to admit, she was pretty good at the basic jitterbug; and she had discovered that when she was dancing with Sam, all her troubles just flew out of her mind, as if each of her worries had wings. It made her want to keep dancing and never stop, but eventually she felt her legs begin to ache and her energy flag. She signalled to Sam that she needed a drink. He instantly stopped dancing and they pushed their way through crowds of young people over to the bar area, which was flooded with Canadian airmen and troops and girls from Poole and Bournemouth, chattering excitedly. Ordering drinks and finding them seats in a quieter part of the dancehall, Sam began to tell Betty about his life back home and how he'd dreamed of being a pilot since he was a small boy.

'I'm due to be posted on active service any time soon,' he continued. 'It's what I've wanted, but now it's coming, I can't lie, I guess I fear it'll be a one-way journey. In my letters home I have to be careful how I word it all. I don't want to worry my family. Oh hey, I'm sorry to be gloomy. Sometimes it just comes out.'

'Do you have a sweetheart in Canada?' she asked. Sam shook his head.

'I was never interested in settling down,' he explained. 'I wanted to travel and see some of the world before I did. Besides, I've never found the right girl. And you?'

Betty found herself lost for words. Wishing she hadn't brought up the subject of sweethearts, she swallowed hard. Not knowing how to tell him about her marriage to Robert, or the impossible situation she'd found herself in, she lowered her eyes and bit her bottom lip before giving him a small smile, trying to communicate that it was all too complicated to explain. Sam read her body language quite differently. Leaning over the table towards her as if he wanted to tell him something, he gave her a gentle kiss, first on the cheek and then on the lips. In her head a voice was yelling at her to pull her head away, get up from that table and walk back to her digs, but her body overruled her head and stayed rooted to the spot. Electrified, her lips tingled as she closed her eyes and kissed him back. Feeling as though she was floating up to the ceiling as the kiss continued, she felt as though she was watching herself from afar, shocked and excited by her own bold behaviour, but knowing deep down that she was playing a dangerous game.

Chapter Thirteen

While Betty danced and kissed the night away, Elsie and William had lain in bed unable to sleep, each of them independently dreading the next day when they had planned to travel to Eastbourne and visit David's mother. White-faced, anxious and sleep-deprived, they now sat together on the train in their smartest clothes, holding hands, fear of the unknown between them like a chasm.

'So much land has been requisitioned for military use,' Elsie said, gazing out of the window at the fields that were now under military control, 'it's a wonder the farmers are able to produce any food at all.'

'Mmm,' said William, not really listening. 'Do you think it's too much for me to just turn up at the door like this? Should I have written first?'

Elsie squeezed William's hand reassuringly. In truth, she had no idea what to expect from David's mother, who neither of them knew anything about. Elsie also had no idea whether, even if David's mother was forgiving of William's dilemma, it would ease his dreadful guilt. But it was worth a try. William needed to do it, to face his demons, and so she would stand by him.

'I think it's better you go and see her,' Elsie said. 'If she has questions, she can ask them, there and then. A letter can be misinterpreted or misunderstood. This is a brave thing to do, William. Very brave.'

She immediately regretted her words. Brave was the last thing he felt, she knew. He sighed and looked away from her, loosening his hand from her grip, and stared blankly out of the window.

She had never meant to patronise him; tears rushed into her eyes and a painful lump in her throat made swallowing difficult. It felt impossible to get it right, but she must never give up. Blinking madly, she felt in her bag for the small tin of barley sugar that Audrey had given her.

'Would you like one?' she said, offering William the tin. 'Audrey had two left over from Christmas. They're still good, bit sticky maybe.'

'I couldn't eat a thing,' he said curtly. For a moment she stared at the two sweets in the tin before putting the lid back on, pushing them into her bag, leaning her head against the seat and closing her eyes.

'Do come in,' said David's mother, Alice Fielding, a tall, elegant woman dressed in mourning clothes. It was typical for widows to wear black for a year to eighteen months after the death of their husband, and for other close family to wear mourning dress for around six months. It had been over a year since David had been killed, but Elsie knew better than anyone that time wasn't necessarily the best healer.

'Thank you,' said Elsie, briefly taking Alice's cool fingers in hers as she and William entered the house. In the hallway, they stood for a moment, disorientated by the darkness. Many of the blinds in the house were drawn – a tradition usually followed for several days after a death to let neighbours know that a family were grieving – but these had obviously been closed for months and the house was dingy and airless. Alice gestured for Elsie and William to go on through to the small living room and sit on chairs that were set around an unlit fire, then quickly scooped up a handful of photographs from the rug on the floor and pushed them under a book.

'Can I get you…?' she said, her sentence trailing off to nothing.

'No, not at all,' said William hurriedly. 'Thank you.'

Elsie scanned the living room. There was little in it: a walnut wood wireless with a little model of a boat resting on top of it, which looked like it may have been made by a child. In the corner stood an upright piano, covered with a dustsheet. On the mantelpiece were a clock and two vases displaying several peacock feathers. Above the fireplace, on the wall, was a photograph of a child who Elsie presumed was a young David. Pulling her eyes away from his joyful face, Elsie studied Alice, whose face was milky white and reminiscent of William's pallor when he spent days on end in the bedroom, refusing to come out. Alice sat down with what seemed like tremendous effort, as if her skeleton ached.

'So,' she said, her face contorting as she tried to control her emotion, 'you want to talk to me about my son.'

Feeling suddenly breathless and trapped by the sheer weight of grief in the room, Elsie longed to raise the blinds and throw open the windows; let sunlight flood the rooms, put on the wireless, fill the vases with daffodils and tulips – but of course she couldn't. When William didn't immediately answer and instead stared awkwardly at his hands as if they held the answer, Elsie spoke instead.

'It's good of you to see us,' she said. 'William has wanted to talk to you ever since he returned home.'

'Returned home' hung like a bad smell in the room and Alice sucked in her cheeks at the tactless words. William silenced Elsie with a glare and she stopped talking at once, giving Alice an apologetic shake of her head. Alice simply nodded slightly and turned to William.

'As I mentioned on the doorstep, Mrs Fielding, I knew your son,' said William. 'We became good friends. He talked of you and of his home often. He said you were a great pianist. I'm desperately sorry for your loss. You must be… devastated.'

Alice remained perfectly still, her back as straight as a rod. She let out a short, exasperated sigh.

'Do you know that when my husband was killed in the Great War, I was not allowed to attend his funeral?' she said. 'I was deemed too emotional by a doctor and was banned from going.'

She directed her words to William and Elsie, but her mind was focussed on a different scene – a moment in time burned onto her memory with a branding iron.

'That's simply dreadful,' said William. 'I'm so sorry to hear that.'

Though Elsie was desperate to make eye contact with William, each of them remained wholly focussed on Alice.

'Just before he died I lost a baby,' she continued. 'So it was just David and me left here together. When the call-up papers came for David, I walked up to the bluebell woods about a mile away from here, out of his earshot, and I screamed. Do you know, there was another mother there from the town doing the exact same thing? We laughed together once we'd finished screaming. But I sensed it then, before he even left, that he would never return.'

William opened his mouth to speak, but Alice got up slowly from her seat and moved to a writing desk in the corner, where she opened a small drawer, reached inside and pulled out a letter. Returning to her chair, she unfolded the letter carefully and cleared her throat. Out of the corner of her eye, Elsie saw William grip the arms of his chair, his nails making indents in the velvet fabric. In the tense silence, Elsie hardly dared breathe.

'Dear Mother,' Alice read. 'It's not so bad here. I'm having an adventure of sorts and making new friends. One chap, William, from Bournemouth, is awfully good at the harmonica. His tunes help lift all our spirits. Don't worry about me, Mother, I'll be fine, I am fine. Love to you always. David.'

Without looking up, Alice placed the letter down on the table with shaking hands. Eventually she fixed William with her pale blue eyes and gave him the smallest smile.

'Thank you, William,' she said, her voice wavering. 'For lifting my boy's spirits.'

Visibly trembling, William rubbed his brow with the back of his hand. With sweat prickling her forehead and her heart hammering in her chest, Elsie didn't know whether to stay quiet or interject.

She desperately wanted for Alice to see and understand the real William, the man she'd fallen in love with, the man David had been friends with.

'You've nothing to thank me for,' he said, clasping his hands together and leaning forward in his chair. 'Mrs Fielding, Alice, I need to explain to you what happened in France. Can you bear to hear it?'

Alice nodded once, lifting a white handkerchief to her mouth with a shaking hand. It was agonising to watch, and Elsie felt waves of nausea pass over her. How unimaginably unbearable it must be for a mother to lose her child.

'We were on an exercise in a small forest, David and I,' William started, every word clearly causing him pain. 'We were making progress when suddenly I came across a young German soldier who was stranded in a hideout. He must have been no more than eighteen years old – he looked as if he could have been as young as fourteen. His skin was freckled, his hair flopped over his eyes. He looked like the kind of kid I was at school with. I lifted my gun to kill him, as we had been trained to do, but that day, I couldn't shoot. It was his eyes. He seemed barely older than a child. I let him escape. David didn't openly judge me, but I knew he thought I had been weak… but then, when I thought he was long gone, the German boy turned back.'

William exhaled and closed his eyes for a moment, as if gathering his strength.

'The German boy turned back and he—' William's voice cracked as he tried to complete his story. 'He shot David in the chest and stomach.'

Tears streamed down William's face and off the end of his nose as he struggled to talk. He didn't wipe them away.

'David instantly collapsed next to me on the floor,' he spluttered, breaking down into sobs. 'I tried to stem his bleeding, but the blood was everywhere and the more I cried out for help, the more distant he seemed to become. In minutes he was dead. I have seen dozens of soldiers die, but when David died, it was as if a light went out. I carried his body as far as I could, but... it was no good, I was not strong enough.'

Alice was in floods of tears now, holding the handkerchief to her face.

'I should have killed that soldier,' William said, tears rushing from his eyes, his mouth contorted and the words coming out in between bursts of sobbing. Elsie glanced at her hands and realised she'd been squeezing her fists so tight she'd drawn blood in her palms.

'If I had shot that soldier, your son David would be alive,' he said to Alice, whose head was bent as she wept. Slipping from the edge of the chair onto his knees, in front of Alice's chair, with his hand on his heart he cowered in front of her.

'I killed him,' he wept. 'I'm so sorry. Your son was a brilliant young man and soldier. He was my friend. I killed him, I watched him die.'

Elsie screwed up her face. It was the most pathetic sight she had ever seen. Her heart felt utterly smashed and her head ached with pity for William and Alice – but she also burned with fury. William had not killed David and for him to say so was utter madness. Suddenly questioning the wisdom of this journey, she stood from her seat, wiped her eyes with the backs of her hands and moved to William to help him up from the floor.

'I think,' she said, to Alice, 'I think we should leave.'

Alice suddenly stood up, knocking over the side table as she moved, and disappeared out of the room. A second later she came back, holding a shotgun.

'Get out of my house,' she said, pointing the gun at William. Elsie whimpered, but then gathered her wits. William continued to cry, his body limp.

'Alice,' she said steadily, 'please, this won't help. We will go. William wanted to tell you how your son died. He didn't kill him. He's suffering himself, he's—'

Alice turned the shotgun to Elsie.

'OUT!' she roared at the top of her lungs, spittle flying from her lips. Elsie grabbed hold of William and more or less shoved him out of the room, into the dark hallway and towards the front door. Before leaving, she turned back to see Alice standing there with her shotgun, a woman wrecked by grief, a mother truly broken. Quickly, she closed the door behind them, grabbing William's hand and pulling him onto the street.

After he'd staggered a few yards up the street on his crutches William pulled on her hand, gesturing that he needed to stop. Leaning his back up against a wall, he covered his face with his hand and slipped down to the pavement, where he sat in a wretched state, his shoulders heaving up and down as he wept. Kneeling by his side, Elsie prised his fingertips away from his face and lifted his chin to face her.

'William,' she said. 'Stop now. You have to stop this now.'

'I can't,' he said, his teeth chattering and his eyes staring into the far distance. 'I can't stop.'

Pure terror ripped through Elsie as she watched her once cheerful and handsome husband quiver and whimper in what she could only describe as hysteria.

'She should have shot me,' he said angrily, lifting his fingers and pushing them roughly against his temple, as if they were a gun. 'If I had a gun, I'd do it myself.'

He almost spat his words at Elsie, pulling his lips over his teeth in a wild, furious state. Lifting his face up to hers, he shook his head before sobbing: 'I'd rather be dead than live like this.'

Her actions were driven by pure instinct. She was usually the last person to resort to violence, but this wasn't a rational decision. She lifted her right hand high in the air and brought it down swiftly across William's cheek, slapping him round the face with some force.

'Don't ever say that again,' she hissed. 'Get up off the floor this minute and let's go home.'

The train journey home was spent in exhausted silence. A group of drunken American GIs burst into their carriage at one point, but they must have read the atmosphere, because they left as quickly as they arrived. With her arms folded over her middle, Elsie gazed out of the window, allowing the rhythmic movement of the train to calm her fraught state. She thought of her father, Alberto, in the prisoner-of-war camp on the Isle of Man and the cheerful letters he sent home to her mother and the twins. She longed to speak to him and see him and talk to him about her life. A single tear escaped her eye and ran down her cheek. She didn't – couldn't – look at William, who she knew was either asleep or pretending to be asleep. She was too raw from everything that had happened to choose the right words.

Back at the bakery, without acknowledging her, William went to help John, while Elsie walked up the stairs to the kitchen with legs that were weighted with lead, gripping onto the bannister and pulling herself up. She could hear that Audrey was in the kitchen, pot-washing. Instructing herself not to put her worries on Audrey's shoulders, she forced a smile onto her face as she entered the kitchen.

'I'm just toasting a teacake,' said Audrey. 'Can I do you one? They're still good. Then you can tell me all about it. And I'll not have you spare me the details. I know that look. You've had a hell of a day, haven't you?'

Elsie nodded, so grateful for the normality of Audrey and the warmth and rhythm of bakery life. With a deep sigh she allowed Audrey to coax the day's horrible experience out of her and was relieved to reveal her deepest fears about William, though she knew it hurt Audrey terribly to hear of it.

'Perhaps he needs proper medical treatment,' said Elsie quietly. 'Barbiturates, or the deep sleep treatment, something like that?'

Audrey sat back in her chair and massaged her bump, deep in thought.

'I don't know,' she said. 'It doesn't seem right for him.'

'I think I should write to Mrs Fielding,' said Elsie. 'To explain.'

Audrey shook her head and smiled warmly at Elsie.

'No, love,' she said. 'That poor lady can't give you comfort, nor can you give her comfort. I would leave that wound alone now. Concentrate on helping to heal William.'

'I thought I was,' said Elsie, tears dripping down her face. Audrey grabbed her hand and squeezed it.

'I know, love,' she said, 'and you have been helping him. Perhaps it's just a matter of letting more time pass. We must be patient and gentle with him, not expect him to snap out of it.'

An image of herself slapping William round the face leapt into Elsie's mind and she flushed with shame, rubbing her palm, which still stung a little from the slap. She should have been more patient and more understanding. But when the person you loved more than anyone else in the world could no longer see the point of living, when most folk were doing everything in their power to survive against the odds, it wasn't always possible.

Chapter Fourteen

Betty felt torn in two. For some of the day she floated around the bakery remembering Sam's sweet kisses, her thoughts lost in the music and movement of the dance, but for the rest of the time she worried about Robert. It was a dead cert that he would come back for her, expecting her to return to Bristol to get on with their life together. He might turn up at the bakery today for all she knew, unkempt in his one and only raggedy old suit, his hands like sandpaper blocks and his stomach empty with no wife to cook him a decent dinner. She almost felt sorry for him. Almost.

'Where's your head today, Betty?' said Audrey as Betty stood staring into space, contemplating her future.

'I expect it's with that Canadian soldier who taught her how to jitterbug,' joked Lily, who was in the bakery helping while Mary played with Joy in the backyard. 'When are you seeing him again, Betty?'

'I-I… don't know,' she said. 'It's all rather complicated.'

'I'll say,' said Audrey with a sympathetic smile. 'But what's life if it's not for sorting out complications? Hey Betty, why don't you invite your Canadian soldier to the bakery for a meal, a smoke and a chat? I'm sure he'd appreciate the welcome. William and Uncle John would like to have another young man around. William is, well, William's… in need of distraction and Uncle John needs a reason to sit down and rest. When he's not baking in the bakehouse, he's mowing the lawns for the neighbours whose men have gone off to war, so they're nice and neat when peacetime comes. Yes, what we need is Sam to come for dinner, to give everyone a reason for a good meal and a relax.'

Lily nodded and smiled and Betty felt she couldn't do anything but agree.

'I'm not sure,' said Betty. 'I'm not sure I should be encouraging him, really.'

'Gracious, you're not encouraging him!' said Audrey. 'Good citizens throughout the town are opening up their homes to military people billeted here. It's common decency, nothing more than that.'

'Okay,' said Betty uncertainly. 'I'll suggest it to him.'

'Invite him tomorrow evening. Right, I better go and get Mary sorted out,' Audrey said. 'I need to check her hair for nits. Apparently, they're going around the school.'

'Ooh,' said Lily, scratching her scalp. 'You're making me itchy.'

When Audrey had left to treat Mary's hair with nit ointment, Betty and Lily worked together to sell off the last loaves of bread before locking up. Lily noticed how quiet Betty was.

'Are you okay, Betty?' she asked. 'You're awfully quiet. Is it something to do with this Sam?'

Betty sighed and placed her hands on the counter. She gave Lily a sideways glance, as if contemplating whether to tell her something, then, clearly deciding against it, shook her head.

'No,' she said. 'It's just my life is getting a bit… confusing. I'm confused.'

Lily watched Betty carefully as her cheeks flushed pink.

'You know, when I arrived here, I was in a fix and nobody in the world but me knew,' Lily said, offering Betty an opening. 'Audrey was so kind when I told her, despite the shame it could have brought upon the bakery. She's helped me no end, unlike Joy's father.'

'So, you're bringing up Joy on your own?' Betty asked, incredulous. 'I thought you had a sweetheart – Jacques?'

Lily sighed and leaned on the counter. Thinking about Jacques made her feel paralysed. She hadn't heard back from him yet but knew that she would. Soon she was going to have to come clean and tell him the truth about Joy. But it wasn't just that worrying her. Deep inside she feared that if he was having ideas about eventually wanting to marry her – if he did accept Joy – is that what she really wanted? Yes, she had strong feelings for Jacques, but she also knew there was a whole other, unexplored, side to her. The more she heard about women stepping into men's jobs, the more she longed to be involved with exciting war work. She loved her job helping refugees learn English, but there were women driving ambulances and working in the shipyards and flying Spitfires. She might be getting ahead of herself a bit here, but there was more to life than becoming a wife. Was it possible to have it all?

'I hardly know him,' she said softly. 'But when we met, we made a connection. I wish I could sit and talk to him, face-to-face, then I'd know where we were and what we were both thinking.'

'You'd think you knew where you were,' said Betty, 'but how can you tell if a person is genuine or not and whether to trust them? I trusted a man and it was a disaster. He took me for a complete fool.'

Lily was taken aback by the vehemence in Betty's words.

'What do you mean?' she said. 'Don't worry, I'm not going to gossip, I promise. I know what it's like to have a burden.'

Betty sighed.

'I'm married,' she said. 'I'm married to a man called Robert, who has also got another wife, Doris. She's been killed in a bombing and now he wants me back.'

'He had two wives?' said Lily, horrified. 'Have you reported him to the police? Men can go to prison for that, you know.'

'No,' said Betty, quickly. 'I've not told anyone but Audrey.'

'Why won't you go to the police?' said Lily.

'Because he's also got three littl'uns by Doris.' Betty sighed. 'What good would that do them? But it leaves me not knowing what to do. If I don't go to the authorities, how can I ever be free of him?'

'Can you divorce him?' asked Lily. 'I know it's uncommon and it would be difficult because you'll be judged, but—'

'But if I divorce him, I'd have to say why,' Betty said. 'And then he'll go to prison and those children won't have a father. He wants me back. Maybe that's the only way. Maybe there's no way out.'

Lily identified with the pain and confusion Betty was feeling. She opened her arms and gave Betty a quick, firm hug.

'There's always a way out,' she said, though in this case she wasn't sure what that way was, 'as long as you've got good friends to help see you through.'

Chapter Fifteen

'…and then there's those poor people in Greece,' said Uncle John, scrubbing his hands in the sink, his white shirt sleeves rolled up. 'They're eating boiled daisies and thistles because they're starving to death!'

Audrey put down the cabbage she was about to chop and leaned her weight on the countertop as John continued.

'…and the poor children are searching for orange peel in the rubbish,' he said. 'Bless their sorry hearts. Oh, it ain't right, Audrey, it's murder by a different name. We can only hope this war is over soon, too many innocent people are tangled up in the whole blasted mess.'

He threw the towel he was drying his hands on down onto the table, folded his arms, sighed and offered Audrey a world-weary smile, a dusting of flour in his eyebrows and on the hair in his nostrils.

'Oh John, I can't stand to hear any more of it,' Audrey said, aware that Mary was half-listening from her spot at the kitchen table where she was polishing the cutlery ready for their guest Sam to arrive. 'It's heartbreaking. It makes you grateful for every crust.'

'You should tell any customers complaining about the National Loaf what I just told you about what some Greek people are enduring,' he said. 'That will keep them quiet.'

Audrey sighed, thinking of some of the sorry sights she saw in the bakery.

'I don't know, John, I think some aren't far off starving themselves,' she said sadly. 'One of our customers, Carol Shaw, that lady from Belle Vue Road, is raising six children on her own in one room on half a shoestring. I always slip extra bread or cakes in her order if she comes in, but I don't know how she gets by, I really don't. Her father was recently prosecuted by the Bournemouth Bench for begging, which doesn't help. He was selling bags of lavender to help her with a few pennies, poor old soul, so now she's really got nothing.'

'I'll make sure she gets some vegetables from the allotment,' said John. 'The potatoes and onions are doing nicely. I'll go up there in the morning to see what I can pull up for her.'

'You should take some time to rest in the morning after working all night, that's what,' said Audrey, pointing a fork at him.

'I could say the exact same thing to you,' he said, with mischief in his eyes. 'Why don't you go and relax, Audrey? You could play bowls at Meryick Park. The women's season has started, and bowls would be the perfect antidote to all this war talk.'

'I haven't got time for bowls!' Audrey said, laughing. 'Besides, they should use the bowling greens for allotments. Mary, please could you run and tell William and Lily that dinner will be in half an hour? That's when we're expecting Sam and Betty. Elsie is working again tonight and Pat too, driving the book van out to the military in the lonely spots.'

'That's my sister for you,' said John. 'Driving people up the wall. No, I can't do her down. She's a grafter all right. In fact, she's the one who should probably be resting! She's not getting any younger and it can't be easy, having a son away fighting.'

At that moment William came into the room. He'd obviously made an effort with his appearance and was clean shaven, but he looked pale and distracted. Audrey felt her heart sink. She hadn't had a chance to talk to him properly about his trip to Eastbourne, but she knew she had to. The problems William had were complex and difficult to treat – but Audrey was sure that with enough home-cooked dinners, fresh sea air, sunshine, love and understanding, he'd get there one day. It was just going to take a lot longer than she and Elsie had first thought.

'I've just checked the ovens, John,' William said. 'The fires are doing fine.'

'Good,' said John. 'Thanks, lad. Let's enjoy our dinner before we get back to work. Now, what can I get you? A Johnnie Walker?'

Lily, Mary and Joy came into the kitchen, Lily chatting about whether Bournemouth would see the usual number of Whitsun holidaymakers that year, and they waited for Sam and Betty to arrive. When they came upstairs, Betty was pink with embarrassment. With her hair newly washed and gleaming, a smidgeon of orange-red lipstick and dressed in one of the frocks Audrey had given her altered to fit her tiny frame, she looked almost doll-like next to Sam, who was a big, strapping lad, with his blond hair swept away from his face and his uniform perfectly pressed. He presented Audrey with a bouquet of roses, which made her gasp.

'They're beautiful!' she said, inhaling their scent. 'My goodness, thank you.'

She was delighted with them, of course, but they must have cost him a pretty penny.

'This is my friend, Sam,' Betty said. 'Sam, these are my…'

'Friends,' said Lily, holding out her hand to Sam. 'Lovely to meet you. This is Audrey Barton, who runs the bakery. William, her brother, Uncle John, little Mary and my daughter Joy.'

Audrey shook Sam's hand and smiled at the young couple, who were a handsome pair.

'It's good to be here,' he said, clearly slightly overwhelmed by the number of people staring at him. 'Feels a lot like home.'

He seemed wistful and Audrey was reminded of when Jacques had stayed at the bakery for a few days of respite. Then, as she did now, she had an overwhelming desire to make sure Sam was made to feel completely welcome. Quickly, she pulled out a chair for him and passed him Uncle John's untouched drink.

'Johnnie Walker,' she said. 'To welcome you. We have brown stew, cabbage and carrots for dinner. I've used all the meat ration so we can enjoy a good meal.'

'Thank you,' he said. 'You're so generous. All of the folk I've met have been so welcoming to us Canadian boys. I think we can be a little too much at times. Loud, at any rate.'

He laughed a hearty laugh and Audrey placed the pot on the table, opening up a lid to reveal a steaming, deliciously fragrant stew. After she'd served it and the dishes of cabbage, carrots and boiled potatoes were passed around, the group tucked into their meal with enthusiasm, murmuring with pleasure.

'Good tucker, as always,' said Uncle John, who had tucked his napkin in his shirt collar. Audrey smiled and lifted a forkful of food to her mouth, but stopped when there was a hammering on the front door.

'Goodness,' she said. 'Whoever can that be?'

'Don't worry about it,' said John, helping himself to more vegetables. 'Just enjoy your dinner. You're eating for three now, remember? I'm joining you for moral support.'

Laughing at John and moving over to the window, she peered under the net curtain and down to the street. Pushing up the sash window, she leaned out and, on seeing a small child, frowned.

'I'm sorry, you'll have to excuse me for a moment. There's a child waiting at the door,' she said. 'Might be one of the evacuees lost, or a little scamp in search of a penny bun. I'll go and see. You carry on. I'm not very hungry, if I'm honest. Dreadful heartburn.'

She made her way down the narrow wooden stairs, her hand resting on her bump, then unbolted the door and was surprised to find not just one child but three standing there, with a man behind them. Running her eyes over the children, she initially thought they must be from a bombed-out house and looking for shelter or help – they were grubby, tired and looked like they hadn't seen a good dinner in a while.

'Can I help you?' she said. 'Are you in need? I've got some stales I will happily give you. Well, they're called stales, but they're perfectly good—'

The man shook his head.

'No, thank you, I'm looking for someone, mind if we come in?' he said, pushing past her into the hallway. 'I've come to see Betty. I know she's here, I saw her walking this way. Where is she? Betty!'

The man called out Betty's name again as he headed towards the staircase, and Audrey realised who this man must be: Robert.

'Oh, I—' she said, trying to work out what she should do, but primarily distracted by the three little children, whose faces told a story of exhaustion. They varied in age. Audrey guessed at around five, three and maybe just over a year, and they must be siblings because they all looked to be cut from the same block. On hearing footsteps behind her, Audrey spun on her heel to see Betty at the bottom of the stairs, leaning her hand against the wall, her face the picture of shock.

'Robert?' Betty said. 'What on earth are you doing here?'

Robert put down the little girl he was holding, who started to cry in earnest, sticking her little arms in the air, wanting to be lifted up into the arms of a warm parent. When Robert ignored her, Audrey lifted her up instead, and hoisted her up onto her hip. She gave the child the door keys she had in her hand to hold and inspect, and the little girl was instantly calmed.

'I told you I'd come back for you,' Robert said, approaching Betty and gripping her hands in his. 'Please, love, I'm sorry for what's happened, but I need you in Bristol. *We* need you.'

Betty's eyes were huge as her eyes ran over the three children's dear little faces. The blood drained from her face and Audrey worried that she might faint.

'We?' Betty said, utterly bewildered. 'Robert, are these your children?'

Audrey watched Betty's eyes fill with tears. There was no denying that Robert's children were adorable little things, all with huge, searching eyes, rosebud lips and wavy dark hair. They didn't seem to know what was happening and the boy hid his head in the overcoats hanging by the door. Then the middle one, another girl, started to whimper. Audrey knelt down to soothe her.

'What is it, petal?' Audrey asked. 'Don't cry.'

'I'm hungry,' the smallest girl said in a tiny voice. 'My tummy hurts.'

Robert faced Audrey, shame casting a shadow across his features, and mumbled something about it being a long time since they'd stopped for toast for breakfast in a café.

'Well, if it's all right with your father, you little ones can come with me,' said Audrey. 'I've some teacakes need toasting and some Fry's cocoa needs drinking.'

The girl in Audrey's arms dropped the door keys and the boy peered out from behind the coats.

'Come on,' Audrey said gently. 'There's nothing to be frightened of.'

'But…' said Betty, anxiously looking at Audrey, her eyes darting. 'What about Sam?'

'Who's Sam?' asked Robert.

Audrey bit her lip as another pair of footsteps descended the stairs and Sam appeared, handsome and wholesome in contrast to Robert.

'I'm Sam,' he said, smiling uncertainly. 'Who's asking?'

'I'm Robert, Betty's husband,' Robert said gruffly. 'Who the hell are you?'

'Husband?' Sam asked, jerking his head towards Betty questioningly. When Betty dropped her eyes in shame and embarrassment, he was taken aback.

'Okay,' he said. 'I'm not sure what's going on here but I think I should be on my way. Thank you, Mrs Barton, for the delicious dinner. Betty, thank you for asking me along. Good night, all.'

'But Sam,' said Audrey, repositioning the child on her hip because the muscles in her lower back were beginning to burn with pain. 'There's no need to take flight, I'm sure Betty will explain what's…'

With panicked eyes, Audrey looked from Betty to Sam, willing Betty to step forward and say something, *anything,* but Betty seemed to be frozen to the spot and unable to offer any explanation. With Robert glaring furiously at her, it was all too much for the young girl, Audrey could see that.

'Well, perhaps you could visit again another day,' said Audrey, showing him out of the door. 'You're always welcome here. Always. Thank you for the roses…'

Sam couldn't leave fast enough, and once she'd closed the door behind him, Audrey sighed, silently reprimanding herself for letting this situation get out of hand. Having Sam to dinner had been her idea. Betty had been reluctant to invite him but Audrey had forged ahead, thinking she was doing the kind-hearted thing.

'Maybe you'd like to explain who the hell Sam is,' said Robert roughly.

'That's rich coming from you, Robert Mitchell!' said Betty, suddenly finding her voice.

'I should think you're the rich one, more like,' he spat. 'Since you've taken my life savings with you!'

'What did you expect me to do?' snapped Betty. 'Survive on thin air? You never let me keep a penny of what I earned!'

'That ain't true!' he said. 'I kept all our money in one place.'

'You probably spent it on Doris,' said Betty. 'Didn't you?'

The mention of Doris's name made the little boy burst into tears. Audrey held on to his hand as he wept into her apron.

'For goodness' sake,' Audrey snapped. 'Put your troubles aside for a moment and consider these three little souls. These kiddies need a good feed and a warm bath. You two can sort yourselves out like grown-ups, while I get these three a toasted teacake and a warm drink.'

Carrying in her arms the smallest, sleepiest child, who had now rested the side of her head against Audrey's shoulder and was sucking her thumb, Audrey led the children upstairs to the warm kitchen and closed the door behind her, giving Robert and Betty time to be alone.

Betty felt shame rinse through her as she watched Audrey lead Robert's three children upstairs and disappear into the warmth of the kitchen where, up until five minutes ago, she had been glowing with happiness. It was her own fault that the evening had been ruined. If she'd told Robert clearly that she didn't want to see him again, then he wouldn't have been here now. If she'd explained the truth to Sam, he wouldn't have been here either. Instead, she'd not been brave enough with either man, which made her just as spineless as Robert, didn't it? It was all her fault. Plonking herself down to perch on the edge of the second stair, on threadbare red carpet, she leaned forward onto her knees and rested her chin in her hand, sighing.

'Do you want to come for a walk?' Robert asked softly, fetching her coat from the hallstand and holding it out towards her. 'So we can talk about this in private?'

Betty shook her head and stared at the hardwood floor for a moment.

'You can say what you want to say here,' she said. 'Besides, you can't just leave your children upstairs in a house where they don't know a soul!'

He leaned against the wall, which was covered in bold floral wallpaper and trimmed with a matching border. For a moment, he seemed defeated, her coat slipping out of his hand and onto the floor.

'I didn't expect you to be carrying on with a Canadian soldier,' he said, 'that's for sure.'

'I wasn't "carrying on" with him,' Betty said. 'He's a friend. I stay near him and pass the time of day with him, that's all.'

Her cheeks warmed at her lie. In truth, she'd been quite taken with Sam and looked forward to seeing him every morning and evening, but Robert didn't need to know that.

'Did you tell him you were married?' Robert said.

'No,' she said. 'How could I? You were married to someone else, until she was killed. I loved you, Robert, with my whole heart, and what we went through in Bristol, being bombed out and seeing our friends' and neighbours' lives destroyed, I thought nothing else could shock me. But when I found out you'd been leading a double life, I questioned everything. Our whole marriage was a sham! I wondered what I'd done wrong, how I could have been a better wife and what I should have done differently to keep you to myself. Then I started to think, it's not me who's in the wrong, it's you! You've lied to me for years. You've told me that we shouldn't have kids, while all the time having your own family round the corner. I can't just forget all that and come back as if nothing has happened.'

Betty was desperate to cry, the weeks of heartbreak and disappointment catching up with her, but, aware that she was in Audrey's hallway while the bakery family were in the kitchen upstairs, probably listening in, she tried her hardest to hold in her tears.

'Why are you here, Robert?' she said quietly. 'Can't you just let me get on with my life?'

Robert was silent for a moment while he stared at his shoes, and then, without lifting his eyes from the floor, he mumbled his reply.

'Doris's sister said she can't keep the kiddies,' he said. 'I don't know what I'm going to do with them. Might have to send them to the Waifs and Strays Society.'

Betty stood up and stared at Robert in astonishment.

'You'd really do that?' she said. 'Just get rid of them? Your own flesh and blood?'

'If you don't come home, Betty love,' he said, his voice deadly serious, 'I might be left with no bleedin' choice.'

'Look who I have here,' said Audrey to William, Lily, Mary, Joy and John, who had cleared away the plates and were sitting at the table, waiting to hear what was going on. 'Three little ones in need of some food and drink. I've just learned their names. This is Dora, Vera and Cyril.'

Audrey was desperate for the three children not to hear Robert and Betty's raised voices. If they'd recently lost Doris, their mother, how confused and frightened must the little mites be feeling already? They had no idea who Betty was. As if reading her thoughts, Mary jumped down from her chair and ran to greet the children, hugging each of them in turn. From downstairs, Audrey heard a door slam shut. She smiled reassuringly at Dora, who, despite being just a baby, was obviously aware of the tension in the air; she was clinging to the strap of Audrey's apron.

'That's kind, Mary,' Audrey said. 'Would you like to show Cyril your jigsaw? How old are you, Cyril?'

'Nearly six,' he said.

'So grown up!' Audrey said. 'William, perhaps you could hold Vera for a moment and I'll carry on holding little Dora, since she's attached herself to my apron! Lily, would you toast some teacakes for the children and I'll put some cocoa on.'

Audrey lifted Vera up onto William's knee and was delighted to see, despite the surreal turn of events, a grin break over his face when the child grabbed hold of his thumbs and giggled.

'She likes you,' said Mary, mesmerised by the younger children. Audrey was about to tell Mary what a good older sister she was going to be when the babies were born, when she was interrupted by Betty throwing open the kitchen door. As she rushed towards a seat and flung herself down, she was as white as flour.

'What is it?' said Audrey. 'What have you done with Robert?'

'He's gone off!' she said. 'He stomped off into the night in a rage.'

'How could he?' said Lily, running over to the window, throwing it open and peering outside. 'What right has he got to leave his kids abandoned in a stranger's h—'

Audrey touched Lily gently on the back to get her attention and said 'Shhh,' sliding her eyes towards Cyril, whose bottom lip was wobbling. 'He'll be back, Cyril. I expect his thoughts are a bit muddled just now. As I understand it, you've all had a lot to adjust to in recent months. Everyone needs a bit of time. He knows you three are safe here with us. Why don't we get the fire going, see if I can't find a story while we're waiting for Dad? How does that sound?'

'I've got some blankets,' said Mary. She dashed out the room and returned carrying blankets from the beds. 'If anyone is cold, they can wrap up in these.'

Audrey eyed Betty, willing her to be as positive and upbeat as the rest of them were trying to be, but she was staring out of the window, looking totally forlorn.

'Betty!' Audrey snapped. 'Why don't you come and sit by the fire? You can have this Johnnie Walker that poor Sam never got round to drinking to bolster you.'

'Oh no, thank you,' said Betty. 'I should keep a clear head. I'll help with the little ones – after all, they're here because of me.'

'They're no burden,' said Audrey, smiling as William held on to Vera's little hands and rocked his knees up and down to gently bump her as if on horseback. 'They're lovely little things. Shall I pour this back in the bottle then? Can't be wasting the stuff.'

'Give it here,' said John, taking the glass and drinking it down in one. 'After this evening's comings and goings, I won't say no to another one neither.'

Chapter Sixteen

Robert didn't come back that night. When it had got so late that the blackout blinds were pulled down, the firewatchers were out on duty and the Mitchell children's eyes couldn't keep from closing, Audrey made up beds for the three of them in with Mary and Joy, with any spare sheets and hessian flour sacks she could lay her hands on. Although they were so tired, they probably could have slept standing.

Audrey then gave Lily and Betty her bedroom to share and, despite their protests, made up a bed for herself in the living room, while William and John went back into the bakehouse to knock back and prove the dough. Before climbing into her makeshift bed, Audrey rubbed some camomile lotion into her sun-kissed cheeks and rested her hand on her bump to feel the reassuring movement of the babies kicking.

'I've barely had time to think today,' she whispered, imagining that the twins were listening. Not that she spoke to them out loud every day, of course, but occasionally she would comment on what was happening around them, imagining that she was preparing them for what their life might be like once they were born. *Born*. Gosh, was it really just a matter of weeks until they arrived? Audrey's heart burned with excitement – and also trepidation. Looking after those dear little Mitchell children made her realise once again the importance of protecting the innocence of children as much as you possibly could. She would be the best mother she could, but it would be a whole lot easier if Charlie was here.

'Oh Charlie,' she muttered before finally turning onto her side to sleep. It was the early hours. 'I wish you were here with me.'

Her thoughts drifted to Betty and the three little children upstairs. She hoped that they would wake up refreshed and that the clanking of the bakery tins at dawn wouldn't disturb them.

Just as she was finally feeling her body relax and the soft, inviting arms of sleep envelop her, the horrible, haunting wail of the siren burst into the room. She woke with a jolt. Unable to sit immediately upright any more, she turned onto her side and pushed herself up to sitting, feeling the skin on her tummy straining over her bump as she moved.

'Gracious me,' grumbled Audrey, her eyes aching as she blinked in the darkness. 'I must have been asleep for all of a second! Must get those little ones up and out to safety.'

Standing in her long nightdress, disorientated and feeling nauseous with tiredness, she knew she must act quickly. There were five small children in the house and they all needed to get to the safety of the shelter as soon as possible. Yanking on her dressing gown, which barely stretched around her these days, and grabbing her gas mask case, she lit an oil lamp and moved into the hallway, where she met Betty, Lily, Mary, Joy and the Mitchell children, wrapped in blankets, tripping over one another in the darkness.

'I'm just in from work,' Elsie said from behind them, still in her clippie outfit. 'Who are all these children? Are they evacuees?'

'In a way,' said Audrey. 'I'll explain. Let's get down to the shelter. Is William in the bakehouse with John?'

Elsie nodded, and Audrey picked up Dora and helped steer the other children out into the backyard and dive into the Anderson shelter for the several hundredth time since the war started.

'Come on, children,' she said, hurrying them in. 'It'll be a squash, but at least we'll be warm, like little birds in a nest.'

A feeling of dread settled into her heart as she realised it was the early hours of Whit Monday and remembered how, during the Whitsun holiday the previous year, Bournemouth had taken a beating from the Luftwaffe. The date had been deliberately chosen to wreak havoc on the town when people would be visiting for their holiday, or at least a breath of sea air. Before slamming shut the door, to block out the terrifying threat of enemy attack, Audrey noticed flares in the sky above the town, briefly lighting up the skyline and German pilots' targets, leaving many people with nowhere to hide. Once inside the shelter, they all stared at each other in desolation as the sound of aircraft and machine guns roared overhead. Audrey's head hummed with worries. Not only did she have all these kiddies to take care of, she needed to get back into the bakehouse before dawn to prepare the counter goods, so that they were ready for 7 a.m. deliveries. She willed the All Clear siren to sound, flinching at the explosions in the near distance. She shuddered, gripping her bump with her hand. What if an incendiary bomb hit the bakery again, as had happened last year? *No point in thinking about the 'what ifs'*, she told herself firmly.

Maybe it was a case of 'wartime' tummy, associated with bad nerves, but a pain ripped through her and she closed her eyes, clenching her teeth to avoid crying out and alerting the others. When the pain subsided, she opened her eyes and wondered if she had any of that stomach powder left that the chemist had given her when she'd described the heartburn and acidity trouble she had. She remembered the logo on the side of the box. Funny what went through your mind in the shelter, when you were exhausted.

'Where's Daddy, Miss?' Cyril asked, interrupting her random thoughts, his enormous eyes shining with fear.

'He's probably in another shelter,' said Mary, taking hold of his hand and squeezing it in hers.

'Yes, she's probably right,' said Audrey, her heart swelling with pride for Mary. 'There's plenty of public shelters in Bournemouth. He will have dived into one of those, I'll bet.'

She hoped she was right and that Robert was safe. Whispering a silent prayer for Robert and Pat and all their family, friends and neighbours, she racked her brain for ways to lift everyone's spirits a little.

'Why don't we sing?' she said to Elsie and Lily. 'Something to get the little ones back off to sleep?'

'"You Are My Sunshine",' said Elsie. 'Jimmie Davis.'

Audrey nodded, noticing how worn Elsie seemed and vowing that she'd find a way to cheer her up tomorrow. Stroking Dora's hair as her eyes began closing, Audrey counted the girls in, one, two, three:

'You are my sunshine, my only sunshine,' sang Audrey, Lily, Betty and Elsie, their voices sweetly soft yet unshakeably strong, a unified sound of defiant hope and love against the backdrop of wartime death and destruction.

When the All Clear sounded just after dawn, the townspeople emerged, sleep-deprived and shivering, from their shelters. Rumour had it that the raids by the Luftwaffe on some areas in the town, including the beloved Upper Pleasure Gardens and along the coast, had been intense and severe. Old Reg had been first with the news, filling Audrey in over the garden fence.

'All those years of growing flowers and pruning in the Pleasure Gardens and it will have been destroyed and burned to smithereens,' reported Audrey to Lily, Elsie and Betty. 'Sewers have been smashed and buildings damaged. It's just causing more disruption for folk. There are craters thirty feet wide and fifteen deep, apparently.'

'Reg said a firewatcher was hurt too,' said Lily. 'Lucky that nobody was killed.'

Helping the yawning, quiet children up to the kitchen, Audrey put the kettle on the range and stared out of the window at the sea, massaging her lower back. Angry dark clouds were gathering over the water, and she squinted at a strip of pale light far away on the horizon. A gap in the clouds perhaps, but far, far, away and well out of reach. She sighed again, before checking her pocket watch and realising that, despite being sleep-deprived, she must get on with the day.

'Lily, Betty, can I leave you to take care of the little ones for now?' she said. 'I need to get my overall on ready for work and Elsie, if you're free, could you give me a hand? Often when there's been a raid like this, extra bread and cakes are needed for the bombed-out at the rest centres and I need to be prepared.'

'Yes,' said Elsie, stifling a yawn. 'Of course. I'll freshen up. There's something I want to talk to you about too.'

Elsie's bones ached and throbbed with tiredness after the uncomfortable night in the shelter, but, as she helped Audrey sort out the buns and put the scones in to bake in the cooling oven, she didn't utter a word of complaint. How could she? With Audrey heavily pregnant but still working like a carthorse, and William and John up all night baking the bread, risking their lives throughout the air raid for the good of the local community, she owed it to everyone to stay upbeat. Inside, though, she was burning to confess to someone what she'd done. As she kissed William briefly on the lips before he went up to their bedroom for a nap, her thoughts went, for the hundredth time, to the letter she'd written and sent to David's mother, Alice Fielding. Despite Audrey warning her not to contact the woman, she hadn't been able to stop herself. Perhaps it was the Italian blood in her, a sense of loyalty to William's good name, or simply caring deeply about someone, but she passionately believed in doing everything in her power to help right a wrong. After their awful visit and despite Alice's intense grief, Elsie was determined to tell her that William was not to blame. Taking a deep breath, she decided to tell Audrey.

'I wrote to David's mother,' she said quickly as they worked side by side in the shop, stacking loaves on the shelves and in a line up against the window. 'I just had to, Audrey. The words wrote themselves, really.'

Audrey stopped what she was doing and bit her bottom lip.

'Has she replied?' she said quietly.

Elsie shook her head and felt a lump forming in her throat. She wished that Alice would reply, but so far, there hadn't been a single word from her.

'What did you say in your letter, Elsie?' Audrey asked tentatively. Elsie couldn't tell if Audrey was annoyed with her – she seemed distracted more than anything.

'I just told her how sorry I was for her loss,' said Elsie, 'and I told her how much William was hurting, that he hadn't visited her for forgiveness, but to share her heartache and grief.'

Audrey shook her head. 'Oh gracious me,' she said, paling.

'What?' Elsie said. 'What is it?'

'I wrote to her too,' said Audrey.

'You never did!' said Elsie, clapping her hand on her mouth.

'I did,' said Audrey. 'I wanted her to know that we all feel her pain. Through William's condition, we feel her loss, but we know that he's suffering too. Poor woman probably feels under attack. Oh gosh, why did I go against my own advice?'

Elsie and Audrey stood for a moment contemplating their actions, until the jingle of the doorbell sounded and a man entered, his face smudged with black soot. Audrey instantly stiffened.

'Robert, you're back,' she said. 'Let me call Betty. She's upstairs. Betty! Where did you go?' She turned her attention back to him. 'You know your three children were terrified last night and didn't know when or if you were coming back? I expect you went off to drown your sorrows in a pint of ale, but I can tell you this for free: ignoring your troubles only makes them worse.'

'Listen, lady,' Robert said. 'I haven't had my nose in a pint of ale or anywhere near one. I went for a walk, to think, and walked miles. Then, on my way back, the siren went off. I found myself near to where the bombs exploded and I got involved in a rescue.'

'Did someone say "rescue"?' asked Flo, who had arrived in the shop with Elizabeth to collect their bread. 'Is this about last night?'

Both women, closely followed by Pat, crowded around Robert to listen to his tale. Basking in their attention, he raised his voice.

'I had to dig out the occupants of a house that had been turned into a crater,' he said. 'In another house a grandfather, father, mother and a boy were in the basement when it was hit. I pulled them all out alive and they went off to the rest centre, but the old man was injured. Their neighbour was an elderly woman and she refused to leave her home – she wanted to stay with her husband, who was paralysed – but eventually, with my help, we got them both out.'

'You were in the right place at the right time, son,' said Elizabeth. 'Thank goodness for you.'

'I'm not all bad,' he said, turning to Audrey.

'I'm sorry, Robert,' said Audrey. 'I shouldn't have spoken to you the way I did.'

Betty came in with Vera, who ran towards her dad and flung her arms round his legs. He lifted her up as if she was lighter than a feather and kissed her cheek. Elsie shared a glance with Audrey, who wore a guilty expression, but her expression changed to one of concern when a police officer came into the bakery.

'There you are,' he said to Robert. 'Finally caught up with you. Sorry, ladies, but this man was seen thieving from a property bombed out last night. He needs to come into the station with me for questioning. Has he been bothering you? Had his hand in the cash box?'

'Thieving?' said Betty, her jaw dropping. 'Whatever next, Robert?'

'I…' Robert stuttered, placing Vera gently back down on the floor. The next moment, quick as a flash, he shoved Audrey out of the way so hard she stumbled backwards and fell to the floor, where she lay spread-eagled.

'Oh Audrey!' said Betty, crouching down by her side. 'Are you all right? Robert wouldn't want to hurt you. I'm so sorry!'

'It's not for you to be sorry,' Audrey managed, wincing in pain. 'He was scared, that's all.'

Everyone was so shocked and concerned for Audrey's welfare that Robert had a clear run to the door, which he flew out of. He legged it down the street. The police officer, an older, overweight chap, ran outside and shouted Robert's name, but he didn't stand a chance of catching him. Elsie knelt down next to Betty to help Audrey up, but she yelped and screwed her eyes shut.

'Is it the babies?' Elsie asked and Audrey nodded, clearly in agony.

'I think they're coming early,' she said. 'Someone will have to watch the shop for me, I can't…'

'Betty and Lily can watch the shop,' said Elsie. Betty nodded. 'I'll help you upstairs. Pat, you've had babies. You'll know what to do.'

Elsie searched Pat's face, hoping that Audrey's mother-in-law was as tough as she seemed.

'Let's get you upstairs right away,' Pat said in a gutsy voice. 'And get these Barton babies born.'

Chapter Seventeen

Left in charge of the shop, Betty stood in the doorway, craning her neck left and right to see if Robert was anywhere in sight or whether, when he realised he'd left his children behind, he might come crawling back. But, apart from Old Reg chalking up a sign for toffee-dipped carrots on sticks as a treat for children who were missing sweets and chocolates, the street was empty.

'Robert Mitchell,' she muttered under her breath, 'you've some nerve running from the police!'

Wondering if any of what he'd recounted about rescuing people in the air raid was actually true, she sighed and went back inside the shop. Scanning the shelves of remaining loaves and the almost empty trays of counter goods, she noticed Cyril eyeing up a carrot cake.

'I'll get you a slice out of my wages,' she said, feeling suddenly desperately sorry for Robert's three children. As Cyril darted off behind the counter, she wondered what was going through their young heads. First, they'd lost their mother and now their father was acting like a criminal!

'Perhaps it's my fault,' she thought, blushing. Perhaps he'd had to resort to crime because she'd taken his money, leaving him penniless? Rubbing her hands together anxiously, she went back behind the counter – and tripped as she almost stepped on a leg. Vera's leg.

'What are you doing?' Betty cried, startled. 'I almost trod on you!'

Hiding behind the counter, huddled together on the floor like fledglings on the branch of a tree, were Vera, Dora and now Cyril, all of them looking up at her with enormous button-brown eyes that seemed to blink with the deliberation of a doll. Stacked in a tower next to Cyril, who had his arm proprietorially over them, were their three gas mask cases.

'Are you our dad's friend, miss?' asked Cyril, which almost broke Betty's heart. She knelt down next to the trio and thought carefully about what she should say.

'Yes,' she said generously, 'I'm Robert's friend. He's had to go out for a while. I'm not sure how long he will be. He's done something naughty and he needs time to work it out, but...'

Dora started to cry and Betty sighed, glancing over at Lily, who was pulling a worried face.

'...but I'll look after you,' she found herself saying, patting the little girl's head. 'Lily, can you manage on your own for a little bit while I find something for these little ones to do? Maybe there's a jigsaw, or you could play in the backyard.'

Betty desperately tried to think of something that these three children would like to do.

'Course I can,' Lily said. 'I'm not due into the library until tomorrow. Mary has Joy outside in the yard, they're playing marbles, so you could all go out there to play. Or better still, why don't you take them down to the promenade for half an hour? Nobody's allowed on the sand at the moment, thanks to the wartime restrictions, but there's a great big pile of sand that's blown up onto the promenade and little ones can have fun in there. You could get them one of Reg's toffee carrots on a stick too. They're a halfpenny each. They'll help you see in blackout – or so he claims!'

Betty nodded, grateful to Lily, and glanced down at the children. They were still in yesterday's clothes, but they were now all smiling. Having never looked after three children all at once, she suffered a moment of self-doubt. Could she properly take care of them?

'I'm not sure if I can—' she started, but Lily interrupted.

'If I can do it,' she said, reading her mind, 'you can. Besides, there'll be another two joining us soon enough. We better get used to taking care of little ones.'

*

Audrey lay on top of the bed in silence, propped up against a pile of pillows, the floral eiderdown draped over her bent knees. Letting the waves of pain roll over her, she held on to Pat and Elsie's hands, refusing to release the scream that threatened to burst out of her lungs. She didn't want to scare any of the kiddies in the bakery, or indeed her customers, many of whom had given birth numerous times, probably while preparing a hotpot for dinner and darning socks at the same time!

Instead, she counted through the contractions and fixed her gaze on the sky out the window. Brilliantly blue, white clouds tore across it as if pulled on a string, the sea breeze rattling the panes of glass in the weather-beaten wooden frames. A fat seagull landed for a second on the windowsill and peered into the room before crying out and flying away. She imagined Charlie, wherever he was in the world, looking up at the same sky and tried to tell him, telepathically, that she was in labour. Perhaps the wind would blow her message to him: that she longed for him to be home, pacing the wooden floorboards in the corridor outside their bedroom door, waiting for news of the twins. This was the biggest moment of their married life and they were hundreds of miles apart. She was determined not to feel sorry for herself – she knew she wasn't the only woman having babies while her husband was away. She tried to channel all their energy.

'You're thinking about Charlie, aren't you, love?' said Pat, holding a cool, damp cloth against her brow. 'Just imagine how happy he's going to be when he comes home on leave to meet his babies. My son's not one for emotional outpourings, but he loves you, Audrey, and he will be a brilliant father when he comes home. Just like his father was to him, bless his soul.'

Nobody said the unmentionable, but Audrey knew they had all thought the same thing, if only fleetingly: *if* he comes home.

Almost every day it seemed someone she knew received a telegram bringing bad news about their son, brother or husband.

'I've wanted this for so long,' she whispered, thinking of all the months and years gone by that she'd hoped and prayed she would have caught, only to discover she hadn't, yet again. 'I can't believe it's happening. I only hope I can be a good mother, like my own mother was before my father died.'

Her thoughts went to her mother, Daphne, in London, and she felt relieved that they had at last made amends. She imagined writing to her as soon as the babies were born and hoped Daphne and her step-father, Victor would be able to visit them – if travel was permitted. Closing her eyes as yet another wave of pain washed over her, her body moving the first baby into position, she breathed deeply and pushed with all her energy.

'That's it, love,' said Pat, dabbing her forehead, where Audrey's hair was stuck to her with sweat. 'You're nearly there. You know some women now are having analgesics in hospital to relieve the pain, so you're doing so well coping on your own. You're going to need a good strong cup of tea after this and then you'll be right as rain.'

From nowhere, the thought of those poor mothers and the new babies who had been killed in the Mill Road Hospital in Liverpool, by a Luftwaffe bombing raid, filled her mind. Audrey felt like screaming again – a blood-curdling scream that would shatter all the windows in Fisherman's Road – but she managed to hold it inside.

'You will be a wonderful mother,' said Elsie. 'You already are, to dear little Mary. These twins will be the luckiest babies in Bournemouth.'

Audrey felt she was dangerously close to losing control of her emotions. Thoughts and feelings bombarded her and a lump grew in her throat when she thought about Mary. These last few weeks she'd been so caring and sweet with Audrey, helping her when she could and doing jobs like polishing her boots, or knitting up baby socks with old scraps of wool. Audrey had no doubt she was going to make a loving big sister to the twins and she would make sure that Mary never felt any different to them; she would soon be a mother of three, all of them equally treasured and loved.

'Oohh,' Audrey said, when, after a moment's reprieve, she felt instinctively that this push was the one. Gritting her teeth, she gripped onto Pat and Elsie's hands and pushed until she felt a great sense of release and the first baby was born.

'Congratulations!' Pat said, 'Your first baby is a girl.'

'Oh Audrey,' Elsie said, tears running down her face. 'I'm so happy for you.'

Pat handed the baby girl to Audrey and she kissed her, crying with pure joy, but she hadn't yet finished. There was another to be born. She breathed through the pain and pushed with every bit of energy she had, and the second baby came into the world to a cheer from the women in the room.

'And this time you have a boy!' Pat said, laughing, her voice breaking with emotion and her face wet with tears.

'Oh, gracious me, what beautiful twins,' said Elsie. 'Double the love.'

Audrey wept with exhausted happiness as both babies were placed in her arms. Checking over every inch of their tiny bodies, she marvelled at the two new lives in her care, silently vowing to love, nurture and protect them with her whole self, forever more.

'What a blessing to have a girl and a boy,' she whispered, as she gazed at their faces in astonishment. 'We must get word to Charlie and tell him we've been blessed with Bournemouth's bonniest babies!'

Glancing up at Pat and Elsie, who had their eyes fixed on the twins and who were grinning from ear to ear, she erupted with joyous laughter, before feeling sudden tears spill down her cheeks.

'Dear me,' she said, wiping her eyes and shaking her head at herself. 'I'm not myself. I'm crying with happiness, I think! I'm sorry.'

Elsie reached for Audrey's hand and squeezed it tightly, while Pat tucked Audrey's hair behind her ears.

'Look what you've just done!' said Pat, gently patting her hand. 'You should be immensely proud of yourself. Time for tea and toast.'

Audrey smiled, overwhelmed with gratitude for her mother-in-law and sister-in-law's help.

'Thank you both,' she said, her voice quivering. 'For all your help and support through this and all the difficult times we've had. I couldn't have done any of it without you.'

Elsie waved her hand in the air dismissively and Pat raised her eyebrows almost up to her hairline.

'Ah,' she said. 'Now what is it that Roosevelt woman says? "A woman is like a tea bag – you can't tell how strong she is until you put her in hot water".'

Audrey laughed through tears, and stared lovingly at the twins, wishing Charlie was there to greet them. She might be a strong woman, but she was weak with longing for her beautiful, tiny new twins.

*

Betty walked back to the bakery with three sun-kissed, happy children, their faces orange from their toffee-coated carrots on sticks, their socks and pockets filled with sand. Half-expecting Robert to be waiting at the bakery, ready to go barmy at her for taking the children off, she tentatively stepped inside and eyed Lily.

'Has Robert been back?' she asked. 'We got a bit carried away in the sand and spotting sand lizards, didn't we, Cyril? He wants to take a jam jar next time to catch one and keep it as his pet.'

Betty ruffled Cyril's hair and the boy looked up at her and smiled. He seemed like a different boy to the one who had arrived with fear and confusion in his eyes only yesterday. This war had prematurely ended many a childhood, but a trip to the seaside had done Cyril no end of good.

'No sign of Robert,' said Lily, breaking out into a smile and pointing to the ceiling. 'But listen, can you hear that noise? The babies have been born! Elsie just dashed down to announce their arrival. One girl and one boy.'

'Oh, that's lovely,' said Betty. 'Twins! Has she named them yet?'

'Not that I know of,' said Lily. 'I'd love to go up and see them. Are you willing to watch the shop for a few minutes? Then you can go up too. I'm sure these three would like to see newborn twins?'

'She probably won't want all of us hanging around,' said Betty, suddenly stricken with panic about what she was going to do with the children now that the babies had been born. 'If Robert doesn't come back, I'll have to take them back to my digs.'

Lily pulled a worried face and popped upstairs to see the babies, leaving Betty alone in the shop. But she wasn't alone for long.

'Is it true?' said Flo, popping her head in through the shop door. 'Has she had twins?'

'Has it happened?' said John, walking in from the bakehouse. Betty nodded and John beamed, wiped his eyes with his hanky and clapped his hands together.

'A boy and a girl,' said Cyril, delighted to be imparting important news. Flo exclaimed with joy. John shook his head, mumbling something about 'double trouble'.

'What's this?' said Elizabeth, her head appearing beside Flo's. 'Has Audrey had the babies? Is she well?'

'She'd had them!' said Flo, nodding. 'A boy and a girl. Ain't that just the best news?'

'I must go and knock round a few of the neighbours,' said Flo. 'They'll all want to know the good news and we've all got bits to bring. Second-hand odds and ends, but they'll come in useful.'

'Did you want any bre...?' asked Betty, but the women had gone before she finished her sentence. She found herself smiling nonetheless – the joyful news of Audrey's twins being born was infecting everyone. When Lily came back down, she popped upstairs with Cyril, Vera and Dora to meet the twins and say congratulations.

'Come in, loveys,' said Audrey, already seemingly back to her normal self. 'Come and meet the twins. I haven't named them yet.'

The only hints that she'd just given birth were a few hairs out of place, pink cheeks and the babies themselves. Cyril went right up close to the twins and gently put his finger in one of the babies' hands.

'Cyril,' said Betty, wondering if he should be doing that, but Audrey winked at her and smiled, as if to say it was all okay.

'Are they real?' said Vera from beside the bed. Audrey and Betty laughed.

'Course they're real,' said Betty, still laughing. 'They've just been born. They were safe and warm in Audrey's tummy and now they're out here.'

'Safe and warm in the bakery?' said Cyril, his big eyes on Betty.

'Yes,' said Betty, her heart going out to Cyril and his sisters. They were sweet kiddies, she'd give Robert that much.

After a few moments, Betty gathered up the children and told Audrey she would be taking them back to her digs at the Lansdowne, since there was no sign of Robert. She also wanted to find Sam to try to explain what was going on. 'We don't want to be under your feet,' said Betty. 'You're busy enough now! Thanks for letting all of us stay last night.'

'You'll do nothing of the sort,' Audrey said. 'I'm going to put a pot of stew on in a minute. We'll shuffle around a bit and then you can all stay here until you find out what's going to happen. I'm sure Robert will come back soon. He probably just needs some time to sort himself out, and while he's doing that, we can take care of you three little dots between us. Food might be a bit simple, but I'll do the best I can with the vegetables from the allotment and we'll never be short of bread. We can all pull together a bit, help each other out. How does that sound?'

Betty beamed from ear to ear, hitched Dora up onto her hip and pulled Cyril and Vera against her skirt. Cyril looked up at her expectantly. She smiled down at him, warmth swelling her heart.

'That sounds wonderful,' she said. 'If you're sure it's not too much. Thank you, Audrey. There's not many in this world with a heart as good as yours.'

'Nonsense,' said Audrey. 'Anybody would do the same. What are we here for, if not to help each other out a bit? That's what I want these two to grow up thinking, anyhow.'

*

Outside, Elsie leaned her back against the bakehouse's brick wall, crossed her arms across her chest, tilted her neck so that her head was resting on the wall and followed the flight of a seagull gliding through the sky. She sighed. Watching Audrey's babies being born had temporarily emptied her mind of all the worries that loomed above her head like a dark cloud. She'd forgotten, for the briefest moment, about the heinous war, and her father stuck in a camp on the Isle of Man, and about darling William's deep-rooted grief and guilt. She'd been caught up with the joy of two new lives coming into the world and was full of admiration for Audrey. All of the girls doing war work were brave as anything, there was no denying that, but women going through childbirth were also brave. Taking on the responsibility of bringing up children to be peaceful, loving and kind humans was so important. A part of her wanted to experience that – to have her own child – but she didn't think William was ready. Should you really bring new lives into the world when the old lives were in such a mess?

'You look like you're away with the fairies!' said William, entering the backyard through the open gate and hobbling on his crutches towards her. He held a letter in his hand.

'Audrey's had her twins, a girl and a boy,' she told him. 'Mum and babies all doing fine.'

'I'm an uncle!' William grinned. 'Uncle William has quite a ring to it.'

He shook his head in amazement, sighed happily and leaned against the wall next to Elsie, leaning his crutch up against it beside him. He turned his head to face her and she turned to face him. Their noses were inches apart, their lips upturned into small smiles.

'I know you wrote to David's mother,' he said quietly. 'She's written to me.'

'William, I—' she started, dread and panic filling her stomach.

'It's all right,' he said gently. 'She wrote in her letter that she thought David would have done the same thing as me, and let the German soldier go. She said she understood how wretched I felt, and that I was one of many men making decisions they should never have had to make. She apologised for threatening us with her gun, which she said wasn't loaded. She said both you and Audrey had written and that I was lucky to have two women who stuck by me, no matter what.'

He laughed and looked down at the floor briefly before returning his gaze to her eyes and kissing her lightly on the lips.

'I just wanted her to understand how you have been affected,' said Elsie. 'That part of you—'

'—died with David?' William finished.

Elsie's eyes filled with tears. 'In a way, yes,' she said, swallowing hard.

He nodded and took her hand in his, turning his gaze to the seagulls swooping across the sky so freely. Together they watched the gulls in silence, their hands linked, united, the faint cry of newborn babies trying out their lungs emerging from the bakery, reminding everyone in the vicinity that this was no time to think about the past or contemplate the future. The twins wanted feeding and by the sound of it, they wanted feeding now. War or no war.

'Shall we go inside?' Elsie asked. 'I'm sure the twins would like to meet you.'

'Yes,' said William, a spark in his eye. 'Let me welcome them to the world, in all its complicated glory.'

Chapter Eighteen

'What about syrup of figs?' said Pat, frowning. 'Or we used to tie a lump of coal round a baby's neck with a piece of string. That might help?'

'I'm not tying a lump of coal round his neck!' said Audrey irritably. 'I can't see how that would help at all – and it might strangle him, for goodness' sake!'

'Oh,' said Pat indignantly, busying herself with pegging out freshly washed baby booties on a short line erected above the kitchen range. 'There's no need to take that tone.'

The first three weeks of the twins' life had passed in a frenzied blur of feeding, crying and napping. The bakery was bursting at the seams with baby paraphernalia passed on from customers; a pram carriage for twins, knitted pram sets, matinee coats, tiny shoes and the ugly but vital gas helmets for babies that were always on hand in case of gas attacks. And two of everything!

Since Betty and the children were still staying at the bakery, after Robert had failed to return, it was a squeeze. Audrey's kitchen, where she was now sitting with Mary and the twins, was piled high with jobs that needed doing: bakery paperwork, washing, darning and Mary's school dress covered with fruit stains that she needed to clean off with lemon juice and salt. The list of things to do was longer than she was tall. She stared crossly at her mother-in-law, who was dressed in her WVS uniform and who, whenever she called in, dispensed more unwanted advice to a bewildered Audrey. Knowing very well that she was only trying to help, Audrey sighed and smiled an apologetic smile.

'Sorry to be so rude, Pat,' she said with an exhausted sigh, gazing at the twins lying together in a Moses basket. 'I've not slept for days, some of the customers are late to pay their bills so I can barely afford to pay anyone and I'm worried sick about Donald. He's not thriving like his sister and this runny nose and cough is worrying me. What am I doing wrong? I thought this would come naturally to me, but it's tough.'

'You're not doing anything wrong at all,' said Pat. 'He might have croup. I think you should get the doctor to take a look at him. He's got a bit of a fever running. Try not to worry about the bakery. Everyone's pulling together and it's all going well enough. Just concentrate on the babies for now.'

Audrey ran her fingertips under her eyebrows as if propping open her eyes and sighed anxiously, before leaning back in her chair.

'Thank you, Pat, you're right. I'll see how he goes,' she said, 'and if he doesn't pick up, yes, I'll take him to see the doctor. Poor little mite, it's such a worry.'

'No word from Charlie?' asked Pat. Audrey shook her head. She'd written to tell him about Donald and Emily, but he hadn't replied.

'I'm sure you'll hear from him again soon,' Pat said. 'Right, I better get going. I'm helping with this book chain and there's a lot to do.'

'Book chain?' asked Mary. 'What's that?'

'Anyone who has any spare books or magazines has donated them for the waste paper drive for the war effort,' explained Pat. 'There's seven chains and each one will be started by the mayor himself and they'll all lead towards the Town Hall. People are leaving their books outside their front gates, so I'm going around to help pick them up. Would you like to help? Audrey, can you spare Mary?'

'Mmm?' said Audrey, distractedly, frowning as Donald started to grizzle. 'What was that?' She picked Donald up and rocked him gently.

'Can you spare Mary?' Pat repeated. 'I could do with some help.'

'Yes,' said Audrey, undoing Donald's top and spotting a little pink rash on his chest. 'Yes, of course I can.'

'Good,' said Pat, stretching her hand out to Mary. 'Let's hope it doesn't rain.'

Audrey didn't notice Mary and Pat leave the kitchen. She was too busy worrying about Donald and the strange cough he had. Holding him in her arms while Emily slept, she walked him to the window, thinking that the sunlight might do him good, but the brightness just made him howl even more. Hearing the crying, Lily came into the kitchen, carrying Joy. In her hand she carried a letter.

'Is he getting worse?' Lily asked, and Audrey nodded. 'Yes. I think I should get the doctor. I'm terribly worried about him. He doesn't seem right. Could you look after Emily for me while I go to Reg's and call the doctor?'

'Of course,' Lily said, pushing the letter into her pocket and biting her lip.

'Did you want to talk to me about that letter?' Audrey said. 'Is it from Jacques?'

'It can wait.' Lily smiled. 'Donald is much more important.'

*

Lily took a seat in the kitchen while Joy played with some wooden blocks on the floor and Emily slept in her basket. It was moments like these when she wondered how on earth she'd got here. Her life had taken an unexpected turn, two years ago, when she'd fallen pregnant by her old boss, Henry Bateman. At the time she'd been working at the Ministry of Information in London and feeling as though she was at the beginning of an exciting career. Now, she was a single mother of a toddler and living with her stepsister in Bournemouth. She enjoyed her job at the library helping refugees with their English, but she knew she could do something much more exciting, like join the WRNS or the WAAF or ATS, given half a chance. There was a drive in Bournemouth to get women to join the services and Lily had been to a WAAF display in the square.

She'd been transfixed and had wanted to join there and then. The trouble was, though, what to do about childcare?

And now, today, a letter had arrived containing another unexpected turn. Jacques had written again – and this time, just as she had suspected, he had asked for Lily's hand in marriage. Unfolding the letter and smoothing out the paper on the kitchen table, Lily read and reread his words. He said life was too short to procrastinate, that he had fallen in love with her when they first met and that he wanted her to be his wife, and for them to share their lives together.

Thoughts tumbled through Lily's mind. Jacques didn't know about Joy – she had yet to write and tell him. And even if he did accept Joy, something in Lily's mind bristled at his choice of words: 'to share their lives'. No matter how much she liked Jacques, a small secret part of her wanted to keep her life for herself and not share it at all. You only got one life and you had to make sure you spent it wisely. Resting her forehead on the kitchen table, she opened and closed her eyes until she was disturbed by Joy tripping over one of the wooden blocks, knocking her head on a table leg and bursting into tears. The sudden noise woke up Emily and she started to cry too.

'Oh, it's all right,' said Lily, trying to soothe both girls at the same time. 'You're going to be okay!'

Lifting Joy to her lap, she shook her head at herself in dismay. What was she thinking of, dreaming of the WAAF and the WRNS? Her life was here, looking after her daughter and helping Audrey. She'd write to Jacques and tell him the truth; Joy was her priority and he needed to know that, and she wasn't going to share her life with someone she hardly knew. Jacques needed certainty and security and an escape, she understood that, but he also needed to be realistic. If they had any chance of having a relationship of any description, they had to know everything about each other first.

Resolving to write to him that evening, Lily decided she would finally tell him everything. No secrets, just the truth, and if he still liked her after that, *then* she would think about the future.

*

Doctor Morris was busy, called out to one emergency after another, so Audrey left a message and decided to contact him the following morning if Donald hadn't improved. Something she'd learned in just a few weeks of motherhood was that babies could be terribly unhappy one minute, then perfectly happy the next, so perhaps he'd be much better by dawn. She tried to reassure herself that this was the case, but that evening, he seemed worse. Despite yawning with exhaustion, Audrey was determined to stay awake while the babies slept, so she could keep an eye on him.

'Come on, little love,' she whispered to him, gently rubbing his back as he coughed and coughed, 'try to rest now.'

At midnight, Lily popped her head round the door and smiled at the sight of Donald asleep in Audrey's arms.

'How's he doing?' she whispered. 'He looks like he's sleeping peacefully now.'

'In fits and starts,' said Audrey in a hushed voice. 'He's been coughing and has a fever, and has barely fed, but I think he's worn himself out, poor dot. I daren't put him down though in case he wakes up again.'

'Can I watch him for you?' Lily said. 'I can hold him while you get a bit of sleep?'

Audrey smiled gratefully, rolled her aching left shoulder to iron out some cricks, but shook her head.

'I can't leave him,' she said, kissing his head. 'I just can't.' She carefully sat down and gestured to Lily to sit down too.

'I thought you'd say that,' said Lily. 'I'll come and sit with you for a while, then.' Before she did so, she draped a blanket over Audrey's knee and Donald's legs.

'What did you want to talk to me about earlier?' said Audrey.

'Jacques has written again,' said Lily. 'And as I suspected he might, he's asked for my hand in marriage.'

'Oh Lily, that's wonderful,' Audrey said, gently stroking Donald's back as he shifted his position. 'I'm so glad for you, but how will it work out with him being in France? Perhaps a long-distance engagement until the war's over?'

'I don't know,' Lily said, looking at her hands and inspecting her nails.

'What is it?' Audrey asked, checking Donald's forehead with her finger and frowning – his temperature was still very high.

'I still haven't told him about Joy,' said Lily, shrugging. 'I think he's getting rather ahead of himself. And…'

Lily paused, tucked her copper hair behind her ear, and Audrey tapped her on the arm to get her attention.

'And what?' she said. 'Come on, Lily, spit it out.'

'I really like Jacques,' Lily said, 'and I can imagine loving him, but it's all this talk about marriage and sharing our lives together. I don't know if it's for me. I know I have Joy to take care of, but I want to have adventures, explore the world and work. I don't want to be stuck at home.'

Audrey smiled at Lily. She was quite a modern girl, really, and Audrey admired her forward-thinking attitude, but she worried about how she would manage with looking after Joy on her own if she never married. If Jacques was understanding about Joy, she'd be daft to let him get away.

'What do you think?' Lily said. 'Am I being selfish?'

'Not at all,' said Audrey. 'You're being sensible and anyway, Jacques needs to be told about Joy before you think any more about marriage. I think that Jacques has had a horrible few years and is desperate for love. Remember when you helped wash his sore feet when he first arrived at the rest centre? You must have seemed like an angel to him. You are an angel – but an angel with a mind of her own and ambitions. Just be yourself, Lily, that's all I can say.'

Audrey was interrupted by Donald coughing again, and this time he vomited a little before seeming to gasp for air. The vomit was faintly streaked with red and the skin of his face had a purple-red tinge.

'Is that blood?' Audrey asked, panic-stricken. 'Oh gosh, Lily, I don't know what to do. I don't know how to help him!'

Terror gripped Audrey as she held Donald in her arms, feeling utterly helpless. Her stomach twisted further when she saw the expression on Lily's face – pure fear. 'Let me see if I can fetch the doctor,' said Lily, her face completely white. 'I'll wake him if I have to.'

Chapter Nineteen

'There's someone here to see you,' Lily said, poking her ashen face round the door.

'Is it the doctor again?' Audrey asked, barely looking up from baby Donald's face. 'Send him in. He's still having difficulty breathing. I'm worried sick…'

Audrey hadn't slept a wink since the doctor had called in the middle of the night and diagnosed Donald with whooping cough. He had recommended a vaporiser and a few drops of Friar's Balsam and said he'd need to be quarantined from the other children in the bakery, but that there was little more he could do. Audrey had known enough children perish from the disease to know that Donald's condition was very serious.

'No, it's not the doctor, it's me,' said Charlie, slowly coming into the room with an obvious limp and removing his hat. 'I've had a stint in hospital and I was allowed home on compassionate leave to see you and the babies. I tried to get word to you, but obviously it didn't reach you…'

Audrey's jaw fell open and her legs turned to liquid as she tried to process Charlie's sudden arrival. Moving towards him and flinging her arms round him, she couldn't hold in her emotions a moment longer and burst into tears.

'Hey,' he said warmly, holding her into his chest. 'Are you going to introduce me to this little one?'

Audrey, still holding onto Charlie, leaned back so that she could study his face. Her eyes, filled with tears, blinked in amazement and she wondered if she was perhaps hallucinating after not sleeping all night.

'Yes,' she sniffed, wiping her nose and eyes and forcing herself to pull herself together. 'This is Emily and this is Donald, your twins. I'm afraid Donald is poorly. Very poorly. The doctor came last night and said he's got whooping cough—'

Feeling the desperate urge to break down into tears, Audrey broke off. She wouldn't collapse in front of Charlie. She had to stay strong, even though it was painfully difficult. Swallowing hard, she continued.

'The doctor has given me plenty of advice,' she said, with a sniff, 'and everyone has been helping around the clock.'

'Can I hold him?' Charlie said, gazing into the Moses basket at Donald.

'Of course, love,' she said, carefully handing him the baby. 'Yes, there. That's right. How much leave do you have?'

'Two days,' he said. 'No time at all.'

They smiled knowingly at one another; their expressions showed their despair at how helpless they were in the face of war, that their lives were no longer their own. In Charlie's big, capable hands, so used to hard graft and, more lately, weaponry, Donald looked as small and fragile as a snowdrop petal. His breath was raggedy and his little chest heaved in and out with every breath. It was a moment before Audrey realised that Charlie was weeping. Tears slipped down his face and onto the baby's head. Audrey gulped.

'Don't cry, my love,' she said. 'I know he will pull through. I believe it in my heart. I'm so sorry to greet you like this. They're such little angels.'

Charlie shook his head, letting out a deep, shuddering sigh.

'He's so small and… and… fragile,' he said. 'He's wholly dependent on you and on the good of people. It's the contrast between this tiny baby, *our* tiny babies, and the front line, I can't get my head around it.'

'No,' said Audrey quietly, not wanting to interrupt.

'I've witnessed the deaths of strong, able soldiers on the front line,' Charlie said, quickly wiping away his tears, 'and in the moments before death, they have called out for their mothers.' Choking on his words, he paused to shake his head before continuing.

'When faced with a sudden, violent, painful death, a man craves the innocent years of childhood,' he said, 'when their mother held them in her arms so gently, just as you are doing.'

Audrey was speechless as she tried to comprehend the men's pain and suffering. Charlie's words moved her deeply and only served to strengthen her resolve to stay by Donald throughout his sickness and nurture him back to health. She and Charlie linked fingers and gazed at Donald as he took raspy breaths.

'Is there a chance that he…?' said Charlie, letting his unfinished sentence hang in the air.

'That he might die?' whispered Audrey, her voice breaking. 'I couldn't bear it, Charlie, so I will not think it.'

Suppressing tears, they sat together on the bed, watching over their son, praying for him to pull through this critical time. Deep down, Audrey knew that there was a slight but real and dreadful possibility that Donald could die – and if that was his fate, she vowed that he would take his last breath safe in the arms of his mother and father. That he would go in love and in peace.

While John, William and the girls worked hard to get the bakery open and running, Audrey and Charlie stayed with Donald, with Audrey occasionally going into the next room to feed and check on Emily, who, thank goodness, had no symptoms of whooping cough. Though they were often quiet, they talked sometimes in soft voices of what had been happening in Bournemouth since Charlie was last home. Audrey told him about Betty and Robert's children – and about how Robert was married to two women, which Charlie couldn't quite believe. She discussed how, once Donald was well enough, she planned to hold a small welcome-to-the-world party for the twins and how she wished that Charlie could also be there.

'Do you think the war will go on much longer?' she asked, holding Charlie's hand. 'Are we any closer to it ending?'

'I don't think so,' said Charlie, with an enormous sigh. 'Not as far as I can see. I wish I could tell you otherwise.'

Audrey sighed and rested her gaze on Donald, who, she suddenly panicked, seemed to be turning blue around the lips. Quickly picking him up from his basket, she held him to her chest and looked at Charlie, wild-eyed.

'I don't think he's breathing!' she said, her heart hammering in her chest as she broke out into a cold sweat. 'Oh Charlie, what shall we do?'

Audrey felt herself overcome with fear. So strong was her terror that she couldn't think straight and felt frozen.

'Come here,' Charlie said, taking Donald from her and bringing his ear close to his son's lips. 'He's got to breathe! Oh, please God, please breathe.'

At that moment Pat put her head round the door and, seeing what was happening, ran towards them and grabbed Donald by the ankles, hanging him upside down and patting his back until he made an incredible spluttering noise. Wiping the phlegm from Donald's tiny mouth as he coughed and struggled to breathe, she exhaled in relief, while Audrey, totally in shock, wept into her palms.

'He's okay,' soothed Pat. 'He's going to be okay.'

'Thank you, Mother,' said Charlie, wrapping his arms around her. 'I thought the worst then, I really thought he'd stopped breathing.'

Charlie moved to Audrey and held her in his arms while she allowed herself to cry. Pat saw to Donald and soothed him until his irregular breathing eased.

'I thought it was dramatic on the front line!' Charlie said, letting out a relieved laugh. 'Are you all right, Audrey love?'

Audrey nodded, but she looked and felt wrecked, after what was one of the most terrifying experience of her life. 'I'm sorry, I'm—'

'You're tired. And you need a cup of tea and a bite to eat,' said Pat firmly, feeling Donald's forehead. 'I'll bring you a sandwich up. I think Donald's fever is abating and his colour is improving, so let's hope this is a turning point.'

'Come on, son,' said Charlie, stroking Donald's tiny hand. 'When I go back tomorrow, I want to know my boy is going to be safe and well.'

Audrey glanced at Pat and didn't miss the wistful smile on her face.

'It's all we want for our sons,' said Pat softly. 'To be safe and well.'

Chapter Twenty

'Shhh,' said Betty, holding her finger to her lips to silence Cyril, Vera and Dora. 'You have to be really, really quiet, like mice who live in a library. Baby Donald is not well and Charlie, the master baker who owns this bakery, is home on leave. The last thing he'll want is noisy children he doesn't even know under his feet. Do you understand me?'

Cyril and Vera nodded, while Dora just blinked and carried on sucking her thumb in Betty's arms. Poor little mites. Since Robert had disappeared, Betty had been taking care of the children at the bakery and they'd had no choice but to accept her as a temporary parent. Betty had barely seen Audrey, who was busy tending to Donald, and felt constantly guilty for her presence in her home. She kept thinking that she should find somewhere else to go but was at a loss to know where. If she returned to Bristol, there was no guarantee that Robert would be there and anyway, with their home bombed out, where would she live? She had no money to pay for a rented room anywhere and she couldn't go to the Assistance Board to ask for help because the children weren't her own – and if she reported Robert for abandoning them, she knew he'd just get into deeper trouble. Despite everything he'd done to disappoint her, she didn't want to completely ruin his life.

'How is Donald?' she asked Pat, who was in the kitchen preparing a sandwich. 'I feel like we're all under Audrey and Charlie's feet here, but I don't know where else to go.'

Pat turned to face Betty with red eyes. Obviously, she'd been crying and Betty felt guilty for bothering her.

'Are we going back home?' asked Cyril meekly. 'I like it here.'

Betty and Pat exchanged glances while Cyril opened his eyes wide in anticipation of the answer. Betty gently patted him on the head.

'We're not going anywhere today,' said Betty. 'Is Donald worse?'

'I think he will be okay,' said Pat, swiping creamed margarine on the bread in a hurry, 'and you mustn't worry. You're doing a good turn by Robert, looking after his kiddies, we all know that. Audrey would never see you without a roof over your head, but what with Donald having whooping cough, you need to be careful these three don't catch it. Actually…'

Pat paused from spreading margarine and lifted the knife in the air while she thought something through.

'I have an idea,' she said finally, returning to the bread. 'I've been putting up some land girls but they're moving on in a week. Why don't you and the children move in with me, to free up some space here at the bakery?'

Betty didn't reply immediately, quite stunned at the Barton family's kindness, which seemed to run through their veins in place of blood. She'd once peeked inside Pat's house when running an errand for Audrey and it was the most lovely, homely home – though, she thought, as a vision of the grandfather clock, collection of antique walking sticks, vases and a cabinet filled with trinkets flashed into her mind, it wasn't exactly a house for little children.

'You won't have to pay me, if that's what you're thinking,' said Pat, putting the sandwiches on a plate and moving towards the door. 'You can earn your keep helping with the chores.'

'Oh of course, I would definitely help,' said Betty. 'No, I was thinking more of all the precious things a lady like you might own and whether these three might accidentally damage something.'

'Don't be daft!' said Pat. 'I'd rather see you all comfortable than protect a vase from breaking. Besides, if Hitler and his cronies invade, no doubt they'll take anything valuable from us straight away. Just look at what happened to the folk in Jersey. The Germans ransacked the place!'

'Do you think they will invade, like in Jersey?' said Cyril, his eyes wide circles.

Betty opened her mouth to answer, but at that moment, Lily entered the kitchen, with Joy squirming and fidgeting in her arms.

'She's hungry,' said Lily, placing Joy on the floor and putting her hands on her hips. 'I haven't had a moment to sort out dinner and I wanted to run this letter to Jacques to the post office before I change my mind. How is little Donald doing?'

'Slightly better, I hope,' said Pat. 'His temperature has dropped a little.'

'I can help with Joy,' said Betty. 'I can do a cold tea for all the children, can't I? With Fry's cocoa afterwards.'

Four faces turned towards Betty, their hopeful eyes shining with happiness at the thought of tea. Dora, still in Betty's arms, pushed her cheek against her shoulder and Cyril slipped his hand in Betty's.

'Oh, thank you, Betty,' said Lily. 'You have a touch of a mother hen, you know.'

With the plate of sandwiches for Audrey and Charlie in one hand and the other on the kitchen doorknob, Pat suddenly spun round on her heels.

'I've just had the most brilliant idea—' she said, but before she could speak another word, the siren sounded its horrible, dreadful wail.

There wasn't room for everyone in the Anderson shelter, so while Uncle John and William bravely remained in the bakehouse tending the ovens, so tomorrow's bread would be baked in time, Audrey saw to it that Pat took baby Emily, Lily, Betty, Mary, Joy and the three Mitchell children into the shelter.

'Be safe,' she called, handing Pat Emily's milk bottle, as anti-aircraft guns echoed in the air. Anxiously, she watched the line of women and children walk out into the garden, gas masks over their arms, pushing through the overalls still hanging on the washing line, and into the shelter door. Imagining them all trying to fit into the small space, with just a flickering candle for warmth and light, she hoped that Emily didn't wake up crying, wondering where she was. Less than a month old and having to hide underground from bombers – how could this be happening? She could only hope that, having lived through the war, the little ones would grow up doing everything they could for peace.

'They'll never get any sleep tonight,' she said to Charlie, helping him move the wardrobe in front of the bedroom window to protect against blast or bomb splinters. 'I hope the All Clear will sound sooner rather than later.'

Cradling a sleeping Donald in his arms, Charlie perched on the edge of the bed and Audrey sat down next to him. Anti-aircraft guns were firing in the distance, and they heard the sound of a bomb exploding and looked at each other in fear.

'Didn't sound too far away, did it?' whispered Audrey. 'Oh Charlie, do you think Donald is through the worst?'

Charlie nodded, staring down at his son.

'I hope so, love,' he said. 'His breathing seems a bit better. What will you do about Emily? She'll miss her twin if they have to be kept separate.'

'Doctor says he won't be contagious for long,' Audrey said, 'so they'll be back together soon enough.'

She gazed at Charlie, burning to tell him how much she was going to miss him when he returned to active service and how she wished they'd become parents in peacetime, so that he could know his children as babies. But, though she longed to spill out all her fears and concerns, she knew it was unfair and unhelpful. This part of his life, at home, was Charlie's respite. These precious memories would have to see him through the next few months – or years – of combat. She would keep her thoughts to herself.

'What do you make of the National Loaf?' she asked him. Charlie pulled a face.

'Can't deny that John and William are doing a good job,' he said. 'But I'd rather bake and eat a Coburg any day of the week.'

Audrey smiled.

'The bakery is running all right,' she said. 'Some of the customers are late with their payments, but that's nothing new, is it?'

'No,' Charlie said, shaking his head. 'But don't let it get out of hand.'

When he was at home, running the bakery, he'd clubbed together with other master bakers in Bournemouth to put an advert in the *Echo* asking customers to pay their accounts, or else the bakers couldn't afford to buy the ingredients. It was a difficult one though – neither Charlie nor Audrey would ever see any of their customers go hungry.

'I won't,' she said, not wanting to worry him with the books.

'Will you write and tell me how the twins are doing?' he said. 'How they change each month, when they start talking and crawling and all that? Even if I don't get the chance to reply? You know I'm not one for letter-writing.'

'Course I will,' Audrey replied, yawning. 'I'll write every detail about them and I'll be sure to tell them everything about you too. Sorry, I'm barely able to keep my eyes open.'

Audrey felt an overwhelming need for sleep wash over her. She had snatched a half-hour here and there over the last few days, but now felt quite poorly with exhaustion.

'You look done in. Why don't you lie down for a while?' Charlie said. 'I'll sit here with Donald. It's quietened down outside, so with any luck the All Clear will soon sound.'

But Audrey didn't want to lie down. She didn't want to shut her eyes and miss out on the last hours of Charlie being home, or to risk sleeping through Donald taking another bad turn.

'I'll wake you if Donald gets bad again,' said Charlie, reading her mind. 'Go on, you'll be no good to anyone if you're starved of sleep.'

She didn't need telling again. Leaning back on the bed, pulling a corner of the eiderdown over her and resting her head on the pillow, she held the image of Charlie and Donald in her mind's eye as she closed her eyes. In seconds, she was in a deep sleep, where she dreamed of nothing and nobody.

Hours later, with sunlight sneaking in around the corners of the blackout blind, Audrey woke, startled and disorientated. Noises came from the shop downstairs, the voices of her regular customers and tinny music from the wireless filtering into the edges of her mind. Sitting upright, with her heart pounding in her chest, she saw that, instead of Charlie, Pat was sitting on the chair by the bed, cradling Donald in her arms, feeding him a bottle of milk. Looking down at herself, Audrey realised she was still wearing her apron from the previous evening. Blinking in confusion, she pushed her hair from her eyes and sat up.

'Where's Charlie?' Audrey said, already knowing the answer.

'He had to go,' Pat said. 'He didn't want to wake you because you were so fast asleep. The air raid didn't go on for long last night, though a bomb was dropped on the racecourse and all those allotments were destroyed. Nobody was injured, thank goodness. Donald seems to have improved. Do you want to get some more sleep?'

Audrey felt a myriad of emotions. Though she felt relieved that nobody had been hurt last night and that Donald was probably through the critical period of his whooping cough, she felt furious that Charlie had gone again without saying goodbye. But at least he'd met the babies – you had to be grateful for small mercies.

'I can't,' she said, steeling herself. 'I've got a bakery to run and two babies to look after, not to mention Betty, Robert's three kiddies, William, Elsie, Mary and Joy and Uncle John.'

'I've had an idea that might help,' Pat said, looking pleased with herself. 'I'll explain it to you later, when you're washed and dressed.'

Chapter Twenty-One

As she walked to the Hotel Metropole to track down Sam and offer him a belated apology, Betty mulled over Pat's idea. While they were in the air raid shelter, Pat had proposed that, between them, they run a nursery from her home.

'You're good with children and are kind-hearted,' Pat had said. 'I qualified as a children's nurse – a long time ago, but I can still remember it all. I'm good at discipline and insist on proper behaviour. I've read about residential nurseries in the papers – lots of women around the country are helping out their neighbours, family and friends while mothers go off to their war jobs. We could potentially look after Joy, Cyril, Vera, Dora and the new twins when they get a bit bigger, to help. Mary too, when she's not at school or helping at the bakery. What do you think?'

Betty felt excited by the idea – she loved little ones – but she still had her shifts at the bakery to do and she wouldn't want to let Audrey down.

'We would take it in turns to watch the children,' Pat said. 'Then you could do your bakery shifts and I could do my WVS work.'

Not knowing how long Robert's children would be with her made it difficult for Betty to make any decisions, but since he'd not been in touch at all since fleeing the bakery, she had to admit to herself that he was a complete bounder. Despite resenting him, she lived in hope that he'd want to know his children were safe, and she couldn't send them into a care home – they were too sweet for that. But what if he never came back? Did she have the capacity and desire to look after them for ever?

'Oh Robert,' she said to nobody, shaking her head at the thought of him in hiding somewhere. 'Don't be a coward. Do the right thing for once!'

Realising that she'd reached the entrance of Hotel Metropole, she suddenly felt incredibly nervous. She'd left it far too long to come and apologise to Sam, but she'd felt too embarrassed and silly for not telling him about Robert to come before now. Besides, he hadn't been able to get away fast enough when Robert had turned up and, she suspected, wouldn't want anything to do with her.

Recognising a friend of Sam's called Jim, who had been at the dance they'd enjoyed together, she walked over to him, her face burning red and her palms clammy. What if Sam had told his friends about her? They'd think she was a dreadful person. Swallowing her embarrassment, Betty smiled at Jim.

'Excuse me, do you remember me?' she said. 'I'm a friend of Sam's. Could you give him a message for me please?'

Jim's face dropped, and he cast his eyes to the floor, pushing his hands into his pockets.

'I'm sorry, miss, but haven't you heard?' he said quietly.

Betty shook her head. 'Heard what?' she said, hardly daring to breathe.

'There's no easy way of saying this. Sam went out on a mission in France, but I'm sorry to say he didn't come home again. His aircraft was shot down over the ocean. He was one of many to have been killed.'

Killed? Betty struggled to stay standing.

'Oh, I…' she started, but was lost for words.

Gently, Jim supported her by holding her elbow and she gripped his arm for a few moments before letting go. Tears dripped down her face. Sam was so full of life, energy and fun. Now he was dead. She thought of the family he'd described in Canada and how he'd tempered his fear in his letters to them so as not to worry them – they'd never see him again.

'I'm sorry,' he said. 'Can I get you something? A cup of tea or something stronger?'

'No,' she muttered. 'No… thank you, I-I must go.'

Leaving Sam's young friend standing in the entrance of the hotel, she staggered back out onto the street, and stood for a moment in the sunlight, trying to take in the news and chastising herself for not coming to see him sooner. She should have come to apologise the day after the dinner at the bakery, not left it so long. In wartime you couldn't assume you had any time at all. If something important needed to be done, or said, it should be done or said straight away.

Curling her fingers into fists, she set off through Bournemouth town centre towards the bakery, all the while thinking of Sam, remembering the way he danced, the line of his shoulders under his jacket, the gentle kisses he'd planted on her lips. As she passed the bomb craters in the Pleasure Gardens and the damaged surrounding buildings with boarded-up windows and flanked by sandbags, she cursed Hitler's crazy greed and his thirst for violence. Men like Sam were dying before they'd even started living to protect the peace, so Betty would do everything she could to help peace prevail – whether that be running a nursery so that women could do war work or volunteering more with the WVS.

Taking the cliff path towards Southbourne, she eventually stopped at the bench on the Overcliff and sat down, staring out to sea. A beautiful day. She realised how fortunate she was to be able to appreciate the sight of the gulls gliding on the thermals, and the sea glistening in the sunlight. Sam would never see this again. Tears rolled down her cheeks.

'Hello,' said Audrey from behind her, making her jump. 'What are you doing here? I thought you were running errands in Bournemouth? I've just snatched ten minutes to bring Donald out into the sunshine. Elsie's watching Emily for me before she goes to work, bless her— Oh no, are you crying?'

Betty bit down on her bottom lip, knowing that she would just cry harder if Audrey showed her any more of her characteristic kindness.

'It's Sam,' she said. 'He went out on an operation but didn't come back. He's dead.'

Clearly shocked, Audrey sat down on the bench next to Betty and held onto her hand.

'I'm so sorry to hear that,' Audrey said quietly. 'He seemed such a nice man. Can't have been more than twenty-one?'

'Twenty-two,' Betty said. 'I don't know how best to honour his memory.'

'We have to carry on helping to put an end to this war in whatever way we can,' said Audrey. 'That's all we can do to honour those who have died. I'm so sorry, Betty, I know you liked him.'

Audrey rested her hand on top of Betty's and, taking a deep breath, Betty forced herself to stop crying.

'You're right and that's what I intend to do,' she said, determinedly. 'Pat had an idea that she and I could set up a nursery at her house. Then, when I'm not working my shifts at the bakery, I can be looking after the children. It might help Lily when she works at the library, and you, to know the twins can be looked after for a few hours while you work at the bakery.'

Audrey sat up straighter and nodded.

'Yes, yes, it would,' she said. 'When Donald is stronger it would be very helpful – but you've already got a lot on your shoulders, what with Robert's children. I still can't believe he left them with you and has disappeared without a trace. What's he thinking of?'

Betty sighed and raised her eyebrows.

'I have no idea,' she said. 'He's a law unto himself, but I've got attached to Cyril, Vera and Dora. I can't very well hand them over to the authorities without Robert's consent. Besides which, I couldn't do it to them. They've already dealt with so much upheaval. I'm at a loss to know what to do for the best.'

Audrey squeezed Betty's hand.

'If you can find it in your heart to take care of them,' she said, 'I will do everything I can to help. They're the sweetest children and I firmly believe that Robert will be back for them one day.'

Betty smiled at Audrey, amazed yet again by her strength and generosity.

'How do you do it?' she asked, as they both looked out to sea.

'Do what?' said Audrey.

'Remain so calm and strong and forgiving,' Betty said. 'I've never known anyone like you. You're a special woman.'

Audrey laughed.

'Get away with you!' she said. 'There's nothing special about me. I feel the same frustrations and sadness as everyone else, especially with Charlie away. I just try to remember to search for the good and believe that if you look towards the sun, the shadows will fall behind.'

Betty smiled and nodded, trying to commit Audrey's words to her own mind. As images of Sam and Robert flashed into her head and feelings of grief and resentment spread through her body, she told herself that she could cope with whatever life next threw at her. *Look towards the sun and the shadows will fall behind.*

*

Walking to her mother's house in Avenue Road, Elsie pushed Emily in the pram, admiring the way the baby girl had her head turned at almost a right angle on the thin mattress. With her arms up in the air, she was the sweetest little bundle, and Elsie felt most excited to be taking her to meet Violet, whose legs weren't up to the walk to the bakery.

'Aren't you just the picture of perfection?' Elsie said, smiling down into the pram, as she paused to correct the knitted blanket that Emily had kicked off.

Earlier, William had helped her wash and change Emily while Audrey took Donald out for some air, and Elsie had been quite taken by how much looking after the baby girl lifted William's spirits.

Seeing the joy on his face as he gently dressed her in her pram suit made her heart swell with hope. For once he'd seemed light-hearted and free from burden and, for a moment, she'd considered turning to him and saying that yes, they should try for a baby, until she remembered her reasons for waiting.

'Mother?' Elsie said as she walked into the house, which, after the bomb damage it had suffered two years earlier, was still half patched up with boards and sandbags. Indoors, it looked in desperate need of tender loving care.

'In here!' Violet called from the kitchen. Kissing her mother on the cheek, Elsie scanned the room. The red floor tiles needed scrubbing and there was a basket piled high with washing that needed doing. A bowl of potatoes and leeks waiting to be peeled and washed sat beside the sink, next to a jar of preserved eggs and a packet of crispbread with 'Wartime Economy Pack' on the label. Elsie made a mental note to return later, after her shift on the buses, to help with the chores. With her cane leaned up against the table, Violet was writing a letter, but put down her pen to welcome Elsie.

'It's a bit of a mess,' said Violet apologetically. 'Your sisters are good, as you know, but I'd rather they were out in the street playing while they can. They've spent so much of the last three years in shelters and rest centres, I want them to enjoy a little of their childhood. So, who have you brought to visit?'

After placing a delicious-smelling fresh loaf and a slice of carrot cake from the bakery on the kitchen table, Elsie lifted Emily, who had just woken up and was waving her arms and legs around, out of the pram and placed her in Violet's arms. Opening her eyes and staring up into Violet's face, she made a sweet cooing noise.

'Oh my goodness,' said Violet, her face lighting up with joy. 'What a pretty little thing you are! And how is your twin brother doing?'

Violet lifted her gaze to Elsie, who smiled and nodded before she replied: 'He's improving. Audrey has taken him out for a walk to get some air. Poor little boy, what a start he's had.'

'I know,' said Violet. 'But let's hope he's over the worst of it. He's certainly going to have a lot of love from everyone at the bakery. How is William, Elsie dear?'

Elsie fell quiet and pulled out a chair at the kitchen table to sit with her mother. She sighed and felt her shoulders sag. Though she tried to be upbeat and resilient at work and at home with William, when she was alone with her mother, she couldn't hide her feelings.

'He's up and down,' she said. She hadn't told Violet that they'd been to see David's mother. William didn't want anyone to know, which made it all difficult to explain, so she settled for a general description of his health. 'He has nightmares about when he was in France and he obviously finds it hard to move on from the front line. The happiest I've seen him lately is when he's helped me look after Emily, or any of the other children.'

'Bless him,' Violet said. 'Are you tempted to have one of your own? You know my feelings about it. You should get on and have a family.'

Elsie shrugged and sighed while Violet gently tickled Emily's cheek.

'But there's a war on,' she said. 'I think we should wait. I'm so busy on the buses and you obviously need more help here.'

Offended, Violet huffed and sucked in her cheeks.

'No, I do not,' she said. 'I'm managing perfectly well on my own, thank you very much.'

Elsie could see her mother was close to tears, so immediately changed the subject.

'Sorry,' she said. 'Who are you writing to? Is this a letter to Dad?'

Violet shook her head, regained her composure and cleared her throat. She moved the letter in front of Elsie so she could read it for herself, then explained what it was about.

'Some of the Italian people who have been interned are now being released,' said Violet. 'I'm writing to everyone I can think of to appeal for your father to be released. After that terrible disaster at sea, I think the government are finally realising that arresting all the Italians was a hasty thing to do. Honestly, when I think about what Alberto's suffered, after all he's done for this country, I'm overcome with rage.'

'Can I help in any way?' said Elsie, sharing Violet's fury. 'I better take Emily back in a minute, but I can write some letters too tonight. There would be nothing better than getting Dad home. You must miss him so much.'

'I do, love,' said Violet. 'He's my husband and he should be by my side, helping us through this dreadful war. Families should be together. Family is the most important thing.'

Elsie promised to help write letters to whoever she could think of to appeal for Alberto's release, then left her mother and walked Emily back to the bakery, glancing down at her sweet face and remembering the look of joy on William's face when he held his tiny niece in his arms. Violet was right: family was the most important thing, and Elsie would do everything she could for hers during this dreadful war.

Chapter Twenty-Two

Later in June, though Bournemouth escaped attack, nearby South-ampton suffered a heavy raid involving fifty bombers, which killed thirty-six people and destroyed 160 homes – and the West End of London and Birmingham were also hit, in a series of devastating raids. It had been almost three years, but it still seemed that the war would never end.

One day at the end of June, Audrey was sitting in the backyard having a five-minute break after the shop had closed. She read the headline: 'Germans murder 700,000 Jews in Poland' and her heart almost stopped. Forcing herself to read on, she learned that in the greatest massacre in the world's history, men, women and children had been killed with poison gas in what the newspaper called 'mobile gas chambers', shot or deliberately starved to death. All this atrocious and devastating news in a small article, on page six.

'Dear God,' she cried, dropping the newspaper on the ground like hot coals. She was so physically revolted and horrified by these cruel and tragic events that she felt hot bile bursting into her throat, and she rushed to the bushes to vomit.

'Hundreds of thousands of defenceless people,' she whispered into her hands that she clasped over her mouth in horror, 'murdered in cold blood, oh heavens no! Why, oh why?'

'Audrey?' came Uncle John's voice from behind her. 'Are you all right, dear?'

Wild-eyed, Audrey turned to face John and pointed to the newspaper on the ground, its pages lifted by the invisible hand of the breeze. Slowly, John picked up the paper and read the story, shaking his head in stunned disbelief, muttering and cursing 'monsters' and 'lunatics' under his breath. Walking over to Audrey, he wrapped his arms round her shoulders.

'It says people – *children* and *babies* – were killed outside their street doors, just shot in the street… I can't— It's an unimaginable, devastating crime, John.' Audrey wept until her throat was sore, and though John soothed and comforted her, his cheeks and neck were also wet with tears. John wasn't one to cry and his obvious distress made Audrey feel even worse. They stood together in an embrace for a long moment, speechless with grief, before being interrupted by Mary rushing into the yard, back from the strawberry fields, where you could pick as many strawberries as you could eat for a bob.

'Audrey?' Mary asked, her smile disappearing from her face. 'What's wrong?'

Mary was closely followed by Betty, Cyril, Vera and Dora, who had also been to pick strawberries and who had mouths stained with pink juice and cheeks kissed by the sun. Audrey sniffed and quickly wiped her eyes, before blowing her nose on her hanky with trembling hands and plastering a wobbly smile on her lips. She couldn't tell Mary the truth – how would she explain such a thing? – so instead she wrapped her arms round the little girl and pulled her in for a hug.

'I'm fine,' said Audrey. 'Have you got plenty of strawberries? You smell like one yourself!'

'We ate hundreds!' said Mary. 'And we picked lots too, to make jam. Here you are. Smell them!'

Mary thrust a basket of fresh, ambrosial red berries into Audrey's hands and, as she sniffed their delectable perfume, Audrey's vision blurred with more hot tears. The aroma took her abruptly back to peacetime when the growers had gone around with their carts laden with fruit ready to flog, and folk had enjoyed bowls of them for pudding, served with lashings of cream and sugar. The contrast between that memory and what she'd just read in the newspaper made Audrey feel dizzy. How could two such extremes be part of the same lifetime?

'They look wonderful,' she said. 'I will make pots of jam out of these, but for now, I think I should take you for a swim at the river. I'm always promising to and I never have time, but today, I'll make time. I'll bring the twins for a breath of fresh air too. Let's get a blanket and a few things together.'

The children all broke out into cheers and laughter and Audrey exhaled, pleased to be bringing a smile to their lips. They had to live for the moment, for heaven knew what tomorrow might bring.

'That's it, Audrey,' said Uncle John quietly, 'keep on keeping on. It's all we can do.'

Inside the house, Audrey tried to pull herself together and take her mind off the dreadful news by carrying out some ordinary tasks. She put the strawberries in the larder alongside the nettles she planned to steam and serve with a knob of butter and a dash of nutmeg for dinner, then fed Marmalade the cat the meat from a cod's head she'd simmered in milk and mixed with bread. Moving upstairs when she heard the babies stir from their nap, she collected two blankets from the bottom of the wardrobe, picked up Emily and Donald, took them outside and got them comfortable in their pram bassinet. All the while, in the back of her mind, she couldn't help imagining how those frightened and innocent mothers must have felt, knowing their children were going to be— She shook her head to rid her mind of the haunting images.

'Ready?' said Mary, appearing by Audrey's side with a wide grin. She was followed by the other children, who were chattering excitedly – and Betty too.

'Yes,' said Audrey, then, glancing at Betty with a smile, 'Looks like we've got our hands full!'

Betty almost had to run to keep up with Audrey, who, deep in thought, was marching along the bank of the Stour to find a nice spot for them to sit down and for the children to play in the water. With the sea out of bounds with barbed wire, railings in the water and other defences, the locals had turned to the river for swimming and it was busy with children playing, with their worried mothers on the edge warning them not to go in too deep. Even though the locals had begged the council to cordon off a safe area of the river for bathing, so far they hadn't taken that step and there had been numerous stories of accidents and near-drownings. But, children needed to play in the sunshine and learn to swim in the summer months, and this was their best option.

'How about here?' called Betty, finding a flattened area of grass where a family had obviously previously been.

'Hmm?' said Audrey, who had seemed thoroughly distracted ever since they left the bakery.

'I said how about here?' said Betty again.

'Okay yes, we'll go here,' said Audrey, throwing down the blanket over the grass, near a shallow incline into the water. 'And children, you must only paddle, unless you're a good swimmer. Who can swim?' She addressed the line of children, who were all racing to get off their shoes and socks. Nobody raised their hand.

'Oh dear,' Audrey said. 'Well, then it's paddling only, and you have two fishing nets between you, so you can catch some tiddlers too. I bought a jar with me, for your catch. Off you go! Dora, you can help me with Emily and Donald. I think we'll lie them on their backs on the blanket, so they can kick their legs around and look up at the sky. You'll like that, won't you, my little darlings?'

While Audrey sorted out the twins, Betty sat down on the blanket with Dora crawling across her lap, and watched the children splash, paddle and laugh in the river. Her head was crowded with thoughts: of Sam, Robert and the nursery she was working with Pat to set up. Pat's house had a coal-serviced copper in which they could boil the nappies; they'd give the kiddies cod liver oil and iron tablets, and a teatime snack of bread and jam. They'd play out in the garden and sing and they'd put games and books in the Anderson shelter, to preclude boredom if they had to go in.

'Can I ask you a question, Audrey?' asked Betty.

'Hmm?' said Audrey, who was staring off into the middle distance and frowning. 'Yes, what is it?'

'It's about the nursery that Pat and I are opening next week,' she said. 'We're only looking after the children and babies we know at the moment, but Pat thinks other mothers with wartime jobs might want us to help them. If they do, we'll probably apply for assistance from the government. Anyway, for now, on the days when I'm at the bakery, Pat will be looking after the children on her own. Do you think that it's too much for her? She could potentially be looking after Joy, Cyril, Vera, Dora and the twins all at once and she seems to get awfully tired sometimes.'

'Pat? Tired?' scoffed Audrey. 'Never! That woman has more energy and drive in her than two women half her age put together. Don't you worry about her. She'll cope with that number of children, no problem. And it's not as if it's an official nursery, open 7 a.m. to 7 p.m. like the nursery that's opened in Bournemouth for the munitions workers – it'll just be now and then, won't it, for our family and friends?'

Betty smiled and nodded but couldn't help thinking about the previous day when she'd been creating a play area in Pat's garden. Pat had been sitting on the deckchair for only a minute before she was in a deep sleep with her mouth wide open. What if she did that when she was in charge of the children?

'You're doing a commendable thing, you and Pat,' said Audrey in a serious voice. 'Enabling women to get on with their jobs will hopefully put an end to this war sooner rather than later.'

'It's nothing really,' said Betty. 'As you said, it's just now and then at the moment, to give you and Lily a break – and me help with Robert's children.'

'That's where you're wrong,' said Audrey. 'There's so much wrong in the world that when someone does something good it should be celebrated.'

Betty thought that Audrey was in a strangely emotional mood and wasn't sure why. She hoped she hadn't had any bad news but she didn't want to pry.

'Talking of celebrations,' said Audrey, 'why don't I make a cake for you to have on the first day you have the children at Pat's? I'm sure all the kiddies will want a slice. It might be fatless, eggless and sugarless, but I'll see what I can do. It will be a way of saying thank you.'

Betty blushed at Audrey making such a fuss, but before she could argue, she realised that perhaps Audrey needed a reason to bake a celebration cake. Maybe she was *searching for the good*, and right now this was as good as it got, just as she had said that day on the Overcliff.

'Yes,' said Betty, watching Audrey stand up, balance Emily and Donald one on each hip and walk them to the water's edge to point out a dragonfly hovering over the surface of the water. 'A cake would be perfect. Never mind about the fat, eggs or sugar, it's the thought that counts.'

Chapter Twenty-Three

The dreadful news she'd read in the paper had had a profound impact on Audrey. From the moment she woke up before dawn, to the moment she fell asleep just before midnight, all she could think about was the children who had unwittingly gone to their deaths before they'd barely begun their lives. Though others would argue that children had no choice but to grow up quickly in wartime and should face the horror, she felt as though she had to do everything in her power to protect the younger generation's innocence and try to give them a sense of normality, showing them love and kindness rather than blinding them with stories of blood and violence. She couldn't do anything for those poor little children who had already gone to their deaths, but for the children she cared for, simple, peaceful things like a game of marbles, a stroll by the sea, a gentle story at bedtime and a slice of a freshly baked cake became more important.

'What'll I put in this cake?' she said to herself, at the end of a busy working day at the bakery. They'd sold out of bread and counter goods early, so she'd had time to check the next day's orders before finding the time to quickly bake a cake, then pop it to Pat's when she collected the twins, who had been with Pat and Betty for the afternoon. Hopefully, it would make a nice teatime treat for them all before they had the deep purple beetroot soup, currently simmering on top of the range, for their dinner.

Opening the cupboards and checking through the ingredients, she sighed. Conventional celebration cakes were something of a rarity these days – due to shipping losses, consignments of dried fruit hadn't come through for weeks, icing sugar was banned and the sugar ration at an all-time low. Though she had a certain quantity of ingredients permitted for counter goods in the bakery, home baking was a different story, and she would have to be creative.

'Apples, carrots and honey,' she said to herself, holding a bowl of carrots in her hands. 'I'm sure I can do something tasty with this.'

Taking down a mixing bowl from the dresser, she placed it on the table and arranged the ingredients around it. She created an apple cake using dried egg, sweetened with carrots and honey and flavoured with cinnamon and cloves.

Waiting for the cake to bake, Audrey took off her apron and used the time to write a letter to Charlie. She wanted her letters to bring him joy, so she described as best she could the smell of the strawberries and the pink stains on the children's faces, and the most delightful moment when Emily and Donald had smiled tiny lopsided smiles for the first time. She finished off the letter by making him a promise to get a photograph taken of the twins, so she could send it to him to keep in his breast pocket, close to his heart. Writing to Charlie made her miss him dreadfully and, with eyes blurry with tears, she put down her pen. Wondering when she could find a minute to take the letter to the post office, she quickly turned her attention to the cake, and pulled it from the oven just in time. 'Concentrate, Audrey!' she scolded herself, inspecting the crust, which was moments away from burning. 'Goodness me! Where's my head?'

Placing the cake on a wire cooling rack, she pressed her fingers to her forehead, where a headache was gathering momentum. She sighed. Her head was in a hundred different places – no wonder it sometimes ached.

*

With the delicious aroma of apple cake wafting through the bakery, William walked to the bedroom doorway to find Elsie sitting at the small writing desk under the window. The late sun fell through the window onto the crown of Elsie's black hair, making it shine like molten tar. When she turned to face him, William was taken aback by how tired she looked – she had grey bags under her eyes and her ordinarily cherry-pink cheeks were pale. Her arms, which were uncovered as she was still in her slip, had grown thinner. Concern rose within him. Had he been too self-obsessed to notice his wife was suffering? She worked such long hours on the buses, or else was helping in the bakery or at home with Violet and her sisters – did she ever get time to rest? Had his nightmares kept her from sleep? He shuddered with guilt.

'What are you working on, Elsie?' he said, coming into the room and resting his hands on the back of her chair. He lifted her hair, which was fantastically thick and soft, and let it fall through his fingers. It was the first time he'd touched her hair for ages and she straightened her back in surprise at the contact. She smiled at him, colour rising in her cheeks.

'I'm writing letters to help free my father,' she said. 'Since Churchill said "Collar the lot" and all those innocent people were interned, there's been an outcry. Now, thousands of internees have been freed, but my father is still not at liberty. Mother and I are writing to whoever we can think of to campaign for his release too. He's not even considered a high security risk, so I don't understand why he's still being held. In his last letter he said he was working in glove-making in the camp, so he's just being used as free labour! I'm finding people to vouch for his character and think it's probably a bureaucratic process or a tribunal we have to go through, but I want to hurry it along and get him home again.'

William nodded, feeling horribly aware of how little attention he'd paid to Elsie's family. He realised he must do more to support her, like a decent husband would.

'You're amazing,' he said, leaning to kiss the top of her head. She turned her face up to his and the atmosphere between them was charged. He had just leaned in to kiss her lips when there was a sharp knock on the bedroom door.

'Elsie? William? Are you in there?' said Audrey. 'Could one of you run an errand for me, please?'

'Coming!' said William, smiling at Elsie, then using his crutches to walk to the door. He opened it to Audrey.

'I'd forgotten I promised to pop up to the Norfolk Hotel because they want to increase their bread order,' she said. 'But I'm also supposed to be taking a cake round to Pat's house for tea and to collect the twins. I was wondering if either of you could take the cake for me and if I can get there later I will, otherwise could you bring the twins home for me?'

William looked over at Elsie, but she stretched her mouth into an upside-down, apologetic smile.

'Sorry, Audrey,' she said, 'but my shift on the buses starts in twenty minutes.'

'I'll go,' said William. 'It's only round the corner and I can get there and back before I'm due in the bakehouse again.'

Audrey looked incredibly relieved and quickly hugged William in thanks.

'The cake is on the kitchen table,' she said and dashed back down the stairs; from the bottom she called up: 'Make sure you have a slice yourself. Thank you again, I won't be late!'

William walked, with the aid of his crutches, to Pat's road, which was just five minutes away from the bakery. As he moved up Fisherman's Road, he waved to, or greeted, the various shopkeepers closing up for the day, carrying on their businesses despite the difficult wartime conditions. With bombproof tape on their windows, sandbags protecting the shop entrances and strategically placed stirrup pumps, war was evident everywhere – not least in his missing foot and scarred face, thought William, catching sight of his reflection in a window.

'Blasted war,' he muttered, wishing for a hasty conclusion. On reaching one end of Pat's road, he looked further up the street for her house, number 30, which he easily identified as it had a beautiful cherry tree in blossom right outside the front window. Deciding to take a slight shortcut and approach the house from the back door, he walked down the alleyway that ran along the backs of the houses. Suddenly he became aware of the smell of smoke. He was puzzled: bonfires were now banned. Not knowing where it was coming from, he used his crutches to help him stand on tiptoe and see over the garden fences. He registered in shock that the smoke was coming from Pat's kitchen window and moved as quickly as he could to her house. Pushing through the garden gate and flying up the garden path to the back door, he was greeted by thick smoke billowing from the window. His heart hammered in his chest and he thought of the children inside. Rattling the back door, which was locked, he called out to Pat and Betty.

'Pat!' he yelled, pulling his coat over his mouth. 'Where are you? Betty! Children!'

From inside the kitchen he could hear the terrified cries of several children – and the faint sound of Betty's panicked voice shouting instructions to Cyril, telling him to unlock the door. Trying to work out what had happened and what best to do, William leaned on his good leg and used his crutch to smash the glass of the locked kitchen door. Pushing his arm through, he fumbled through the smoke to reach the key in the door, which he unlocked, letting the door swing open. He was immediately forced back by flames leaping from the floor and curtains. He was temporarily paralysed by a flashback to the flames that had devoured the truck he'd driven in France when it was hit by a bomb, killing all the passengers. He took a deep breath, then, covering his mouth, peered through the smoke to see the group of children huddled together around the pram bassinet in which Emily and Donald were lying. Then he noticed that there was a person collapsed on the floor – Pat!

'Hang on, children,' he said, turning back and searching the garden for something to use to extinguish the fire. Thank goodness for Pat being prepared in case of incendiary bombs – there were several buckets of sand lined up outside. In many streets housewives had emptied the buckets and used them for spring-cleaning, but thankfully Pat had done the right thing.

Hurling the buckets of sand onto the flames, William wrapped his jacket round himself and charged into the kitchen. He scooped up the crying babies in both arms, gathered the children and took them to safety in the garden, before half-carrying, half-dragging Pat, who was murmuring incoherently, out as well and putting her into the recovery position on her side.

Running back inside through billowing grey smoke, he called out to Betty, who he could hear hammering on the other side of the kitchen door. Turning the key in the lock, he flung it open to find Betty in a hysterical state. Throwing her arms around William, she burst into tears, sobbing while he led her outside to safety too.

A neighbour was there. 'I've sent a message to call for an ambulance for Pat,' she said. She had covered Pat with a blanket. 'Are the rest of you all right?' she asked.

'Yes, yes, I think so,' William said, turning to Betty, who fell down onto the grass. 'What happened, Betty?'

'It was my fault,' said Cyril, his huge eyes brimming with tears. 'I locked the doors. I thought, when there was a fire, you were supposed to keep windows and doors closed, in case the flames got out.'

'But not when you're inside!' William said, but quickly softened his tone. 'Don't worry, little man, it's not your fault. You were only trying to help. It's not easy to get things right when you're in a panic. I know that better than anyone.'

Cyril gave William a sad little smile and William ruffled his hair.

'Pat was stoking the fire so we could toast some teacakes and she had a faint,' the boy explained. 'She knocked the guard over and some of the fire fell onto the rug and it started to burn, so fast, and then the flames caught onto the curtains.'

'I was in the other room,' said Betty. 'When I smelled fire and heard the children crying out I went to help, but the door was locked. I didn't know what to do. Thank heavens for you, William.'

By now, the ambulance and fire officer had arrived to put out the fire and a first aider was giving Pat medical attention. Though she was woozy and complained of pains in her chest, she was able to hobble to the ambulance to be taken to hospital for a check-up. After she had gone, William and Betty checked over all of the children to make sure they hadn't inhaled too much smoke but, out in the fresh air now, they seemed well.

'What's going on?' said Audrey, who had appeared at the garden gate, her face stricken with panic. 'Has there been a fire? Where's Pat?'

Rushing over to the children, she threw her arms round them and then checked the twins, who were happily cooing. When Betty explained what had happened, Audrey's jaw dropped in horror.

'Gracious me, what a shock for you all,' she said. 'William, thank goodness for you!'

'That's what I said,' said Betty. 'If it wasn't for William I dread to think what might have happened. He caught it just in time. He's a hero.'

'I'm no hero,' said William, paling as the enormity of the situation began to sink in. What if he'd walked the other way? Would he have made it in time?

'Yes, you are,' said Audrey, 'and I won't hear otherwise. Come on, everyone, let's get you back to the bakery, get you cleaned up and give you a slice of cake. I'll come back later to sort out Pat's house. She won't want to arrive home to singed curtains and black walls.'

'I'll help too,' said Betty. 'It's the least I can do. I should have made sure she was feeling well when I noticed she was getting tired. I hope she'll be all right.'

'That I'm sure of,' said Audrey. 'My mother-in-law is a strong woman. She always puts up a good fight, whatever life throws at her.'

Chapter Twenty-Four

Pat was discharged from hospital two days later, diagnosed with low blood pressure. Betty was one of the first to visit her at home, bringing her a small bunch of wild flowers picked from the clifftop. When she arrived, Pat was sitting in the kitchen, nursing a cup of tea.

'Looks better in here,' said Betty, admiring the work Audrey and Uncle John had done at lightning speed. Audrey had replaced the curtains and Uncle John had given the smoke-damaged walls a lick of paint and opened all the windows to air the rooms.

'Bless them,' Pat said. 'I don't often say this about my brother, but he's a good egg. He always looked out for me when we were children and nothing has changed.'

Betty filled a small vase with water and placed the flowers in it before joining Pat at the table.

'So how are you feeling?' she said. 'Did the hospital give you anything?'

'Look at these,' said Pat, lifting the hem of her skirt to show Betty the sturdy knee-high compression stockings given to her by the hospital, along with a tonic to take daily. 'Aren't they dreadful? It's a good job that my husband is a long time dead! They're to avoid me having a pulmonary embolism, would you believe. Apparently, they're being given out to some older folk now as people have died after sitting for too long in air raid shelters!'

Betty grinned at Pat. She was a remarkable woman. She never showed any weakness and kept a stiff upper lip, forging on with energy and determination.

'I don't suppose you'll be wanting all the children in the house again any time soon,' said Betty as Pat poured her a cup of tea.

'What?' replied Pat, outraged. 'Codswallop! Of course I do. I'll be right as rain in no time at all. While I'm recuperating, I can read to the children and tell them stories. I might need some naps, when they have their naps, and in time perhaps we can get someone else involved for a few hours during the day. I know a lovely girl who helps with the WVS. She's got a little one too. Come on, Betty, where's your determination? Let's not fall at the first hurdle! You need some help with Robert's children too. You can't shoulder that all on your own.'

Betty shrugged and sighed. There was still no sign of Robert, and no word from him. It was as if he'd disappeared into thin air.

'I admire you for looking after his kiddies and I can see you're attached to them and them to you,' said Pat, 'but what will you do if he comes back?'

Betty had no idea what she'd do. Though she endlessly played the scenario through in her mind, she didn't know how she'd react if it happened for real.

'I don't know,' she said, staring out of the kitchen window at the bright flowers growing in Pat's garden. 'It's not something I can plan for. Part of me thinks he's not fit to take care of them, but another part thinks he loves his kids and I fear that the reason he hasn't come back is because something must have happened to him. Whatever the truth is, those children need someone. In my mind they're orphans, just like I was when I was a child. I went into an orphanage in Bristol when I was three and it was a cold, unloving place. I couldn't do that to them.'

Pat gently placed her hand over Betty's and patted it.

'You're a good girl,' she said, 'with a kind heart, and I'm glad to know you.'

Betty looked up from her tea and smiled, warmth and gratitude filling her heart. Getting up to put the cups in the sink, she remembered what she had in her bag. Pulling out the *Bournemouth Echo* newspaper, she turned to the right page and placed it on the kitchen table in front of Pat, smoothing down the pages with her hand.

'Pass me the magnifying glass, will you?' Pat said, pointing at the dresser. 'It's in the drawer.'

Betty opened the drawer and saw the magnifying glass on top of a bundle of photographs. On quick inspection, she realised they were of Audrey and Charlie's wedding – with both bride and groom looking elated, about to cut an intricately iced cake, no doubt made by Audrey herself. Gently closing the drawer, she handed Pat the glass. Standing over the other woman's shoulder to reread the article, she smiled as Pat tutted and exclaimed, the words and image magnified by her glass.

'Whatever next?' Pat said, turning to Betty and raising her eyebrows spectacularly high. 'This is one for the family album.'

*

Uncle John handed Elsie the newspaper article that he had cut out.

'Get that framed,' he told her, 'and hang it above your bed, so William is reminded of the good man he is.'

Elsie smiled. Taking the newspaper clipping, she scanned the words and images. Under the headline 'Hero rescues women and children from burning building!' the article went on to describe William's heroic act, as witnessed by Pat's neighbour, who was heavily quoted throughout the piece. Pat, described as a 'forthright woman with high standards', was reported as collapsing in the kitchen with an undiagnosed health problem, while six children aged five and under almost perished in the fire.

'Brave wounded soldier Private William Allen, discharged from active service after having his right foot amputated, acted heroically when he broke into the burning building, battling flames to rescue the women and children,' Elsie said and grinned at John, who was nodding in agreement. Next to the article was a photograph of William in his military uniform – they must have requested it from his regiment.

'What's this?' said William, coming into the bakehouse to start work mixing the dough.

'It's about you being a hero,' said Elsie, handing him the clipping. While William scanned the words, John busied himself with going up into the flour loft to shift the sacks of flour. Lost in a cloud of flour dust, he didn't see William's eyes glass over.

'It wasn't like that,' he said, quietly. 'I'm not a hero, Elsie, I just love all those kiddies and the babies. My niece and nephew were in there. I had to get them all out – anyone would have done the same thing.'

'They wouldn't,' said Elsie. 'You were a brave man. You deserve this praise.'

'I didn't do it for the praise,' he said, rolling up his sleeves, preparing to work.

'I know,' Elsie said. 'You did it for the children, which is why I've been thinking about what you said a few weeks ago, about us having one of our own.'

Instantly, William stopped what he was doing and looked up at Elsie with hope in his eyes.

'What are you saying?' he said. 'I thought this wasn't the time.'

Elsie shrugged and smiled at him.

'When is the right time?' she said. 'There's nothing stopping us trying, at any rate.'

Leaning against the bakery table, he hugged Elsie and lifted her up off the floor, squeezing her in a tight embrace. In a fit of giggles their lips met and their long kiss was only interrupted by a cough from Uncle John, who, back down from the flour loft, looked embarrassed.

'Don't mind me,' he mumbled, making to leave the bakehouse, but William laughed and put Elsie back down on the floor.

'Come on, John,' William said, grinning. 'We better get this dough mixed and the ovens fired up before Elsie here gets me too distracted.'

Picking up an empty hessian sack, William gently whipped Elsie's bottom with the soft fabric, making her laugh. She picked up a handful of loose flour and threw it over William's head, giving his hair a pale coating.

'You young things!' said Uncle John, shaking his head in mock despair. 'I don't know.'

Chapter Twenty-Five

It was the middle of August when a letter for Lily arrived at the bakery. Reeling from the news that 6,000 mostly Canadian troops had attempted to seize the German-occupied port of Dieppe, and almost seventy per cent of them had been killed, the bakery family were trying to keep their spirits up. Lily, who had been motivated by the United Women's Recruiting Campaign, which was encouraging women to join one of the three services, was trying to discover whether she could join up or do more war work while also looking after Joy when the letter came.

When Freda the post lady handed the letter to her, with an apology because it had fallen onto the floor of the post office and almost got lost, one glance at the handwriting told her it was from Jacques. Her heart pounded in her chest in anticipation of reading his words.

'Can you spare me for a few minutes?' she said to Audrey, who she was helping in the shop. 'It's from Jacques. I'd like to go to the clifftop to read it, if you don't mind.'

'Of course, you go,' said Audrey. 'Take your time, we're not busy.'

Walking towards the clifftop, clutching the envelope to her chest, Lily's thoughts turned to the letter she'd sent to Jacques weeks earlier, revealing the truth about her pregnancy and decision to lone-parent Joy. She'd also written about her dreams of leading an adventurous, exciting life, be it during wartime or, indeed, when peacetime hopefully came again. In no uncertain terms, she'd told Jacques that if they were ever to have a relationship, they needed to get to know each other properly first. Heavens, if her experience with Henry Bateman had taught her anything, it was not to rush into anything with a man. But had her words been too harsh? Knowing that Jacques had been to hell and back, the last thing she wanted to do was destroy his hopes and plunge him into despair. Arriving at the bench on the clifftop, she sat down on the edge of the seat.

'Gracious me,' she said aloud, her stomach doing somersaults and the letter burning a hole in her hand. 'What on earth will he say?'

Her hands trembling, she opened the envelope, her mind drifting back to the day she'd applied Germolene antiseptic ointment to the cuts and grazes on Jacques' tanned back, and the way he'd held her that night as they danced at the Bournemouth Pavilion. Finally opening the letter, she scanned his words, a joyous smile breaking out onto her lips as she read.

Dear Lily,

The day that I met you in Bournemouth, when you so kindly bathed my painful feet at the rescue centre, I fell in love. I fell in love with your spirit, intelligence and good heart, which shines through in your recent letter. It's this same spirit that has led to your brave decision to have your baby and look after her alone despite being abandoned by that philanderer. It's this spirit that craves adventure. It's this spirit that puts me in my place and tells me to be patient and to get to know you before proposing marriage. I admire you and long to be a part of your life. When the war is over I want to see you again and meet Joy. I do not want to own you or control you. I do not wish to dilute your life – only enhance it.

During this war I have lost my best friend at Dunkirk, as well as many other men I grew to know and respect. Their losses make me want to live bolder and brighter than I ever dared. Please, write to me of your dreams and ambitions, and I will write to you of mine. In these desolate war years, I cannot think of anything lovelier than that.

Yours,

Jacques.

'Oh Jacques,' she gasped, reading the letter through again and sitting back on the bench, staring out at the view of the sea and Old Harry Rocks in the distance. She couldn't have hoped for a better reply. He was accepting of everything she'd said. Unlike her stiff, strict and disapproving father, Jacques didn't judge her actions or think of her behaviour as shameful – he seemingly wanted her to be nobody else but herself.

With a grin on her face and joy in her heart, she stood to return to the bakery, excited about telling Audrey her news and writing a reply to Jacques to tell him of her hopes and dreams. Walking away from the cliff through the yellow gorse, back to the path, she looked up at a seagull soaring through the clear sky, wings fully outstretched. And just like that gull, after reading Jacques' letter, Lily too felt she was flying.

*

'Do you know what one of the customers told me today?' said Audrey to Elsie as they worked together in the yard. 'That a woman in Belfast keeps a baby elephant in her garden, not much bigger than this one! The zookeepers thought the elephant was at risk of being killed in a raid, so they evacuated her from the zoo and this kind lady offered to take her in. That does tickle me. I can't stop thinking about it. Imagine looking out of the window and seeing an elephant in your yard, drinking out of a tin bucket!'

The bakery was now closed, and the two women were out in the yard, Elsie running sopping-wet overalls through the mangle and Audrey pegging them out on the line to dry, the sea breeze whipping up their hair and skirts like boat sails.

'How funny!' said Elsie, tucking an escaped curl behind her ear. 'I wonder what they feed it?'

'I can't imagine,' said Audrey. 'Vegetables and fruit, I suppose? Broken biscuits? Do you think it has a ration book?'

Audrey chuckled as Elsie collapsed into fits of giggles, but her attention was grabbed by Lily suddenly bursting through the garden gate, clutching a letter in her hand. From the expression on Lily's face, the letter held precious good news. Audrey couldn't stop from beaming herself.

'What is it, Lily?' she said. 'You look like the cat that got the cream!'

'Wait until you hear this,' said Lily, an enormous smile spreading across her face. Audrey and Elsie exchanged happy glances and listened in stunned silence as Lily read out the letter.

'That's an amazing letter,' said Audrey softly. 'I'm so very glad for you, Lily.'

'I told you he was a good one,' said Elsie, giving Lily a hug.

'You did,' said Lily, holding down the material of her dress in the breeze, 'but I needed to know for sure. The last time I trusted a man I got into a whole lot of trouble.'

'You mustn't be so hard on yourself,' said Audrey. 'You thought you were in love with an available man, you weren't to know Henry was engaged to be married! The scoundrel! Anyway, Jacques is a different kettle of fish entirely.'

'That's right,' said Lily, 'and now I feel like I've been granted a second chance at love. Love the way I want it to be.'

'That's such heartening news,' said Audrey, placing the pegs in the washing basket and resting her hand on Lily's shoulder. 'Now I hope you can enjoy getting to know each other through your letters. You know my Charlie doesn't like writing letters, so I'm grateful for a few lines, but Jacques clearly enjoys it. Keep this letter safe, Lily love. It will lift your spirits during the troubled times.'

From nowhere, Audrey felt tears burning in her eyes and she busied herself with scrubbing the back step. Sometimes the strength of her longing for Charlie startled her, creeping out of the shadows like a big black spider, but she would never show her gut-wrenching sorrowful feelings to Elsie and Lily, nor anyone else for that matter.

What good would that do? As she struggled to pull herself together, her thoughts were interrupted by Elsie clearing her throat. Audrey looked at Elsie and watched a blush creeping up her cheeks.

'Talking of trouble,' she said, dropping her eyes to the floor and squeezing her hands together, 'I've got something to tell you both.'

Audrey stood up straight, glancing at Lily, who quickly folded up her letter and pushed it into her pocket.

'What is it?' Lily said.

Elsie eyed Audrey and Lily. Then the wind suddenly banged the gate shut and she jumped. Audrey held her hand against her heart and rolled her eyes.

'Out with it, Elsie!' she said, walking towards the gate to close the latch.

Elsie blushed and held her hand to her stomach.

'It's very early days, but I missed my monthlies,' she said, quietly. 'I was regular as clockwork before, so I think I've fallen and I can't stop from telling you. William is really excited. I think becoming a father might be the very thing to help him.'

Audrey felt overcome with emotion. Raising her hand to her mouth, she couldn't control the tears popping into her eyes.

'That's wonderful news,' said Lily, throwing her arms round Elsie.

Audrey quickly dried her eyes. 'Oh Elsie, it really is the best news,' she said. 'Gosh, I don't know what to do with all this good news. It's a joy.'

Audrey hugged both Elsie and Lily, elated by their good news, wishing with all her heart that Charlie was there to share it. Before the war, she would have rushed into the bakehouse to tell him, throwing her arms round his neck and giving him a happy peck on the lips. Oh, how she longed to see Charlie again: to hold him, to talk to him about the twins, to cook him a proper dinner, to know he was in the bakehouse working away on the bread while she worked in the shop. Simple, honest, ordinary things – the basic ingredients of their married life.

Chapter Twenty-Six

August ended after fifty-six air raid sirens had sounded in Bournemouth, and September began. Blackberries, elderberries and rosehips ripened on the hedgerows and golden leaves fell from the trees. The hazy warm summer days became bright and crisp, and long evenings were spent inside with the wireless on, knitting gloves for the harsh winter that was predicted. The hard-working bakery life went on, with Audrey at the helm, juggling her new role as a mother of three with running Barton's. Life wasn't easy for anyone, but Elsie was dismayed to notice that Audrey's usual optimism even in the most dire situations had dimmed. She had somehow withdrawn a little, rather as if she'd thrown a blanket over herself. The customers wouldn't have noticed, but Elsie did. Knowing that Audrey rarely spoke about her personal feelings, Elsie left it for weeks before she reached out, but when she found Audrey in the kitchen one morning, rereading the brief letter she'd received from Charlie months before, she felt she couldn't leave the subject alone any longer.

'Audrey?' Elsie said. 'What's on your mind?'

Audrey quickly put the letter down and plastered a smile on her face.

'Nothing,' she said. 'I was just thinking about Charlie.'

Elsie nodded and smiled, wondering if she'd had news of Charlie but not told anyone. She wouldn't put it past Audrey to keep news to herself so as not to burden anyone else.

'You must miss him dreadfully,' said Elsie. 'Especially now you have the twins. Have you had word of him again?'

Elsie held her breath when she saw Audrey's bottom lip tremble. She reached out for her sister-in-law's hand, curling her fingers around her palm.

'Do you want to talk about it?' she asked.

Audrey bent her head and a few moments passed before Elsie noticed the other woman's shoulders were silently heaving and tears were dripping onto her lap. Leaning towards her, she put her arms round Audrey's shoulders and hugged her. In all the time they'd known one another, Elsie had never seen Audrey so vulnerable.

'Oh, I'm so sorry, ignore me,' said Audrey, sniffing. 'I'm being silly and self-indulgent. No good crying! How daft I am.'

Audrey pulled away and started to dry her eyes, but Elsie gently took hold of her wrists.

'Audrey, please,' she said, 'you are always the strong one. Always here for everyone at the bakery, giving out advice and helping people. You were there for me when I needed you. Why don't you talk to me about what's bothering you?'

Audrey shook her head and sighed. Reaching into her pocket for her handkerchief, she dried her eyes and blinked.

'It's nothing more complicated than the war – and the simple fact that I miss my Charlie more than there are words to describe,' she said, her voice flat. 'The twins are growing so quickly, and they don't know their father. I'm normally good at thinking the best and living in hope, but just lately I can't shake this feeling that something has happened to Charlie. I've been having dreams, horrible dreams, about him dying in agony.'

She paused and shook her head, rolling her eyes at herself.

'That's the truth of it, Elsie, and I'm no different to the hundreds of thousands of other people in this country missing their loved ones,' she went on. 'We are all in it together, and we must never, never give up, I know that. I don't know what's got a hold of me. I suppose I dread the twins never knowing Charlie.'

Elsie smiled in understanding, racking her brains for ways to lift Audrey's spirits.

'Have you told the twins much about Charlie?' she ventured. Audrey stood up and walked over to where the twins were sleeping in their crib, shaking her head. Now almost four months grown, Donald and Emily were beginning to roll over from their backs to their fronts, strengthening their necks by trying to arch their backs, making noises that sounded like the beginning of real speech. Gazing down at their sleeping faces, Audrey was quiet for a moment before she replied.

'In all honesty, Elsie, I haven't,' she said, her voice faint. 'I don't know why. I suppose I'm worried I'll cry in front of them! That wouldn't do. I have to be strong.'

'You *are* strong,' Elsie said. 'Why don't you, once a day, every day, talk to the twins about Charlie? Tell them every detail about him, Audrey, share every story you cherish – and even those you don't. That way, they can begin to get to know their father, even while he's away.'

'Yes,' said Audrey, with a small smile. 'Yes, you're right, I should do that.'

'I've another idea too,' said Elsie. 'You said that you wanted to get a photograph of the twins taken for Charlie. Why don't you get on and organise that so he has a keepsake? If you leave it too long, the war will be over!'

Audrey lifted her head to face Elsie and gave a gentle laugh, shaking her head at herself.

'Thank you,' she said, reaching for Elsie's hand and squeezing it, 'I must keep on keeping on and not let those dark thoughts get the better of me. Being down in the dumps won't bring Charlie home sooner or bring an end to this blasted war. Thank you, Elsie. Thank you for listening.'

*

From that day on, when Audrey bathed the twins in a tin bucket in the kitchen sink, she talked to them about Charlie. While Emily and Donald splashed happily in the shallow water, pumping their chubby little arms up and down in excitement, Audrey started at the very beginning. She began with the day she'd first met Charlie, there at the bakery, when, new to Bournemouth, she'd come to Barton's looking for a job to help support herself and William. She racked her brains for every detail she could remember, from the blue shirt sleeves Charlie had worn and the blond hairs on his freckled forearms to the way his eyelashes and brows were coated in a light dusting of flour. She recounted the vigour with which he whitewashed the bakery walls and the sound of his laughter as he chuckled through the fabric of the tea towel he'd wrapped over his nose and mouth to protect his lungs. She spoke of his favourite food – a cone of cockles in vinegar from Mudeford Quay – and the old folk song he whistled while washing his face in a basin full of cold water after his shift in the stifling hot bakehouse. She retold the stories of their marriage and relished every memory, hoping that Emily and Donald were listening, but not minding too much if they weren't. In truth, she looked forward to those quiet moments spent with the babies, talking about their father, her one true love. It was a precious time to be together as a family, in heart and mind if not in person.

The photograph was arranged for a Sunday afternoon, when there would be time for Audrey to dress the babies in their finest baby clothes. Emily was in a yellow knitted dress, matinee jacket, bonnet and booties and Donald wore a pale blue knitted romper suit.

'Where would you like us to be?' Fred, the elderly photographer from Walton and Sons Photographers, said after shaking hands with Audrey in the bakery shop. 'I think we should probably be outside. It's a beautiful day.'

Audrey smiled at the old man, who had kept the family business going in studios located above a sports outfitter in Southbourne High Street, despite his sons joining up. He'd been so sweet when she'd gone to see him and explained that she wanted a photograph to send to Charlie. Film was rationed, so Audrey was able to order a maximum of two photographs, and she'd arranged for him to take one of the twins and another of everyone at the bakery, standing in front of the shop. She planned to frame and hang the group photograph on the bakery wall, alongside those of Charlie's ancestor Eric, who started up the bakery, and one of Charlie looking handsome in his bakery whites, taken years previously.

'Yes, outside would be perfect,' she said. 'Thank you, Fred. I hope the twins smile for you!'

'Children and animals are notorious for not doing what you want them to do.' He laughed. 'But we'll be all right.'

Gathering everyone together, Audrey couldn't help but feel Charlie's absence more strongly, but she did her best to hide her feelings. It was wartime – everyone was missing someone.

As William, Elsie, Betty and the three children, Lily, Joy, Mary and Pat tried to organise themselves in front of the shop window, Audrey realised that Uncle John was missing.

'John!' she called, and he hurried outside with a half-jog, half-walk, dressed in full bakery whites and making everyone laugh. 'Here I am,' he said.

Once the photograph of Emily and Donald, in Audrey's arms, had been taken, Fred shuffled people around to make a prettier line and then returned to his camera and tripod on the pavement. Various friends and neighbours had gathered to see what was going on – and a small boy kept darting in front of the family to try to get in the picture.

'Get out of it, you scamp!' shouted Uncle John. The boy didn't do it again.

'All right, everyone,' said Fred, positioning himself behind the camera. 'After the count of three, smile!'

There was a hush while they waited for Fred to begin counting and Audrey juggled a wriggling Emily in her arms, while to her left Pat held Donald.

'One,' Fred called. 'Two—'

And just before the count of 'three', out the corner of her eye Audrey spotted the familiar figure of a man limping down Fisherman's Road towards them. Turning her head sharply to the left and rapidly blinking to see more clearly in the bright sunlight, she gasped. Just as Fred called 'three' her jaw dropped and she staggered backwards, her perfect astonishment captured on film.

'Charlie!' she whispered, before breaking away from the line and running towards him. Throwing her arms round his shoulders, she pushed her face into his chest, hardly able to believe what was happening.

'I can't believe you're here!' she said, looking up at Charlie, who leaned over to kiss her firmly on the lips. 'I've been so worried, I've had these awful thoughts that you were in trouble, that you had been killed! Oh Charlie!'

'I'm alive and kicking,' he said. 'Just a bit hungry and injured. I've got a bit of leave until this heals up.'

Charlie indicated to his left knee and lower leg, which were bandaged. A moment later and he was swamped by handshakes and hugs and cries of disbelief; and when Audrey finally calmed her racing heart and got around to noticing, Fred the photographer had gone.

'Come inside, Charlie love,' she said, slipping her arm through his, 'and I'll make you a sandwich.'

Fred delivered the photographs to the bakery the following day. The picture of the twins was perfect because they'd both smiled at the right time, though Emily's bonnet had slipped a little. The group shot had captured the exact moment that Audrey spotted Charlie. Her mouth was open and her hand on her heart, her gaze tracked by Pat and John, who were also looking away from the camera. As she laughed at the image, she could have no idea that the photograph would be kept on mantelpieces for generations to come, with people pointing at her and asking who or what had she seen, the story becoming family folklore. She didn't think of the future at all, just of the now.

Although she had only ordered two photographs, there was a third in the packet. Slowly, she pulled it out of the sleeve and, holding it to the light, took a sharp intake of breath. It was the most beautiful photograph she had ever seen. The image captured two lovers locked in a sweet embrace, their bodies urgently pressed together, reunited after the torturous separation of war, expressions of pure and utter joy written on their faces. The photograph was of Charlie and Audrey Barton, together again.

A Letter from Amy

Dear Reader,

I want to say a huge thank you for choosing to read *Telegrams and Teacakes*. If you enjoyed it, and want to keep up-to-date with all my latest releases, just sign up at the following link. Your email address will never be shared and you can unsubscribe at any time.

www.bookouture.com/amy-miller

I've so enjoyed writing this book and, from my research and reading, continue to be amazed and inspired by how women coped in wartime against the backdrop of war, with their loved ones away from home and lives changed in an instant, with the delivery of a telegram. One thing that really struck me was the sense of community. From sharing rations to giving emotional support in times of bereavement and helping with childcare so that mothers could do their war jobs, women's support for one another seemed to know no bounds. I hope that you, the reader, feel that Audrey, the main character in the book, embodies this strength and generosity of spirit. Whatever life throws at her, she keeps going.

I have tried to base events around those that happened in Bournemouth and the wider world during 1942, but there are some fictional events. Though the location of the bakery exists in reality, near the cliff in a beautiful part of Bournemouth near where I live, I have changed street names.

I hope you loved *Telegrams and Teacakes* and if you did, I would be very grateful if you could write a review. I'd love to hear what you think, and it makes such a difference in helping new readers to discover one of my books for the first time.

I love hearing from my readers – you can get in touch on my Facebook page, through Twitter, Goodreads or my website.

Thanks,
Amy Miller

AmyMillerBooks

@AmyBratley1

Acknowledgements

Building on research I did for the first book in the series, I am continually grateful for M.A. Edgington's book, *Bournemouth and the Second World War, 1939–1945* – a brilliantly researched and detailed documentation of exactly what happened in Bournemouth during the war years. I'm also greatly thankful for the Heritage section in Bournemouth Library, where I enjoyed studying the archived *Bournemouth Echo* from 1942. As for the previous books, in terms of the baking content, I am grateful for conversations I had with John Swift, of Swifts Bakery, and team members at Leakers Bakery, Cowdry's Bakery and Burbidge's Bakery, as well as various relatives of wartime bakers, including Anita and Betty. I am also indebted to the residents of the Bournemouth's War Memorial Homes, who gave their time to share memories.

Other books that have been extremely helpful are *Wartime Britain 1939–1945* by Juliet Gardiner; *The 1940s Look,* Mike Brown; *We'll Eat Again,* Marguerite Patten OBE; *Home Front Posters of the Second World War,* Susannah Walker; *A Baker's Tale*, Jane Evans; *Bread: A Slice of History*, Marchant, Reuben & Alcock; *The Wartime House*, Mike Brown and Carol Harris; *Eating For Victory*, Jill Norman; *Make Do and Mend*, Jill Norman; *Wartime Women*, Dorothy Sheridan; *The View From The Corner Shop*, Kathleen Hey; *Spuds, Spam and Eating for Victory*, Katherine Knight; *Reader's Digest The People's War*, Felicity Goodall and *The Ministry of Food*, Jane Fearnley-Whittingstall.

I'm also indebted to online resources, including the incredible personal stories told on the BBC People's War website, an invaluable archive of Second World War memories, written by the public and gathered by the BBC, as well as the many images captured by photographers during the war – one of which inspired the final scene in this book. Heartfelt thanks to everyone who has recorded and archived valuable information over the years, making it possible for me to delve into a remarkable period of history and write this book.